PLAY TABLA

A Manual for the Banaras Style of Tabla Playing

Frances Shepherd and
Sharda Sahai

Trentham Books

First published in 1992 by Trentham Books Limited

Trentham Books Limited
Westview House,
734 London Road,
Oakhill, Stoke-on-Trent,
Stafordshire ST4 5NP

British Cataloguing in Publication Data
A catalogue record for this book is
available from the British Library.

ISBN: 0 948080 27 2

Designed and typeset by Trentham Print Design Ltd, Chester and
printed in Great Britain by Bemrose Shafron Ltd, Chester.

FOREWORD

TABLA PLAYING is a highly developed art form. Tabla players for generations have been introduced to their art systematically through a time-tested set of teaching material. This material is orally imparted and so has not always received the attention it deserves in the West. This manual is an attempt to make widely available a teaching system that is used in India and has produced many professional tabla players of the Banaras school over several generations.

Play Tabla is an introductory text to the art of tabla playing and Indian rhythmic theory. It follows the method of instruction used by members of the Banaras school of tabla playing. Explanations on how to play the main tabla strokes are illustrated by photographs of the hands of Pandit Sharda Sahai. Simple technical details are explained as they occur. All the pieces given as examples in this manual are from the traditional tabla teaching and tabla performance repertoire and are in tintal (16 beat time-cycle), the most important time-cycle in Indian classical music. The book uses the notation system devised by Pandit Vishnu Narayan Bhatkhande.

Students who have little or no access to a teacher of tabla will find the information in these chapters immensely helpful. The book is designed to introduce beginners to the art of tabla playing and to help them develop the correct playing technique. Students with limited opportunity for formal instruction will find it helpful in developing an analytical approach to their technique and their understanding of rhythmic theory. It is suitable for students of any age.

The key to success for a tabla player is regular practice of the right material using correct technique. Thus, in order to obtain the full benefit of this manual, all pieces must be memorised and the instructions for practising followed faithfully.

Indian languages are written phonetically. So there is variation in the English transliterations of Indian words. We have italicised the first time they appear in the body of the text. Translation into English almost always follows the first use of an Indian word, and sometimes successive uses as well. The meaning and correct pronunciation of these terms are given in a glossary at the end, which also has a scheme of transliteration. Tabla stroke names are marked with diacritics as appropriate throughout the text.

We are very grateful to Gillian Klein for her encouragement and editorial help, to John Eggleston for his patience, and to Jack Dobbs for his useful suggestions. Our special thanks to Yogesh Dattani and Yael Offenbach who took the photographs, and to all our students who have helped us indirectly to develop the descriptive and instructional methods used in this manual.

Contents

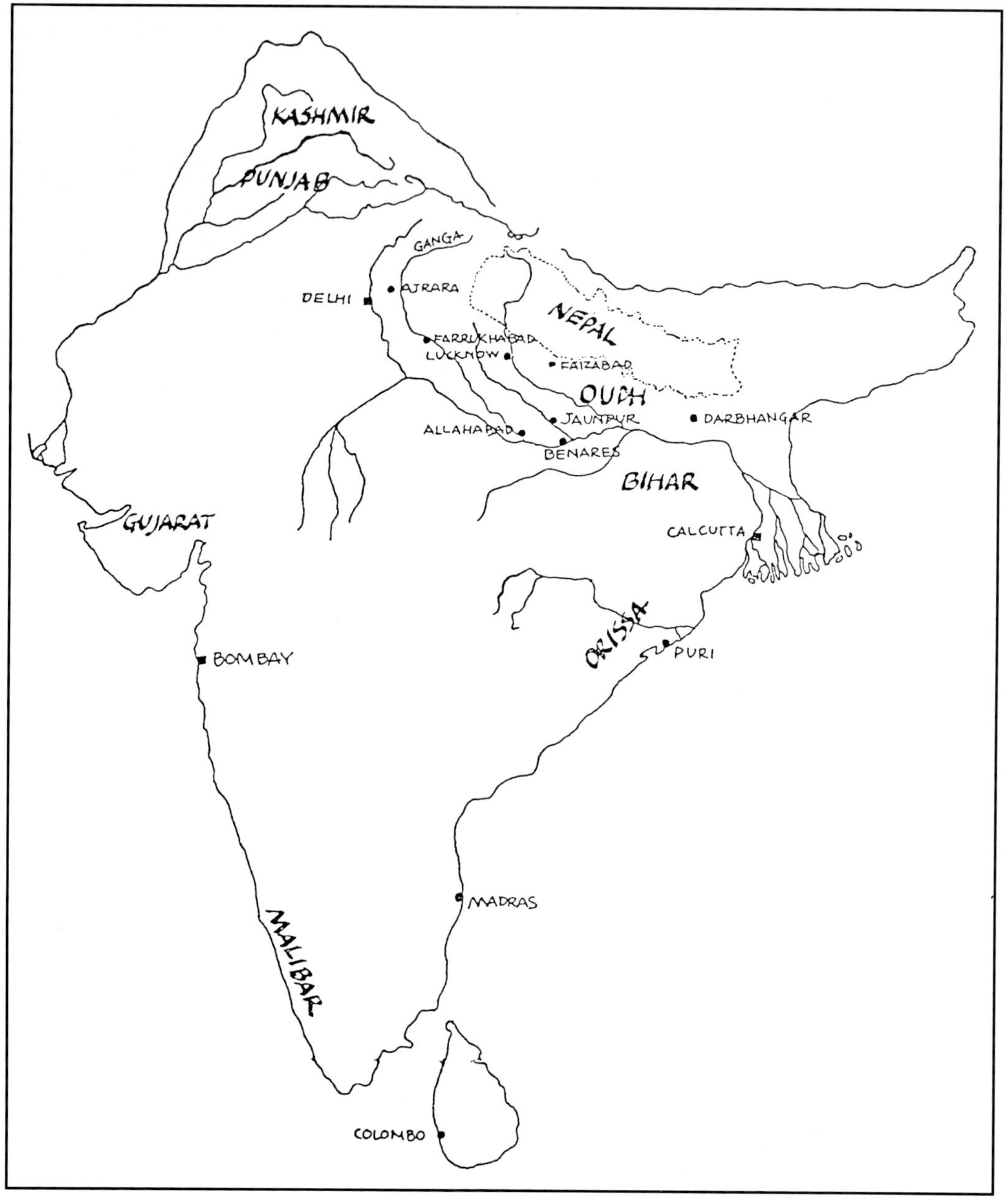

Figure 1

1. Brief history

The most important percussion instrument of North India today is the tabla. It is heard in all spheres of music-making from classical to folk. It is the instrument on which percussion solos are performed, and it is the most important instrument of accompaniment for vocalists, instrumentalists, and dancers.

There are many legends about the origins of the tabla. A popular account of its origin says that the tabla was created by a famous *pakhāwaj* player, Sidhar Khan Dhari. The pakhawaj is a barrel-shaped drum also used in classical music (see Fig 2). Sidhar Khan lived during the first half of the 18th century and was a court musician to Mohammed Shah (1719-1748). Many of his compositions are in the tabla playing repertoire today. It is said that Sidhar Khan became very angry at losing a music contest. In the argument that ensued between the rival musicians, his pakhawaj was chopped in half with a sword, and thus the first tabla was created.

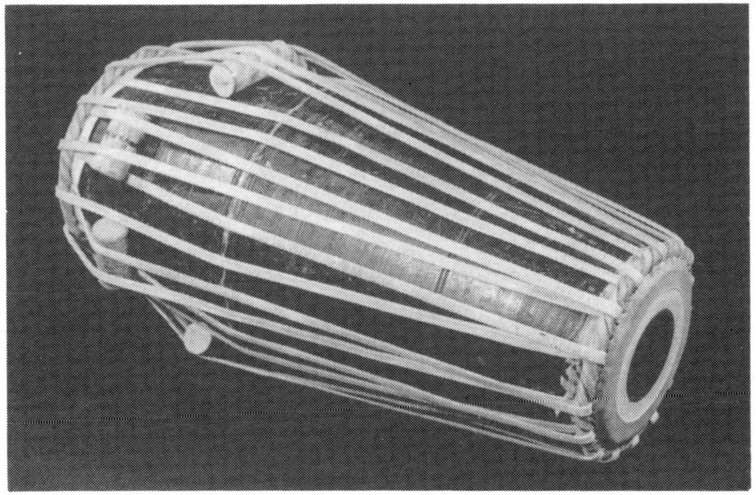

CHAPTER I
The Tabla

Left: Fig 2: The pakhawaj is a barrel-shaped drum also used in classical music.

Right: Fig 3. Whatever its origins, the earliest pictorial evidence of the tabla in its present shape is to be found in paintings of court life in the 1700s.
(Photo credit: Victoria & Albert Museum)

The tabla is also said to have been an invention of the great poet, scholar and musician, Amir Khusrau, who lived in Delhi in the 13th and early 14th century. This is doubtful, as Amir Khusrau wrote extensively about his achievements and inventions but never mentioned the tabla among them. In the ancient temple sculptures of India, instruments similar in appearance to the tabla are depicted. They show a musician playing a pair of conical drums of identical size with his hands. They are very similar to the *dahinā* of the tabla pair. The bowl-shaped *bāyā* has many counterparts in ancient Indian clay drums and until recently the baya was made of clay. The name 'tablā' most likely has its origins in the Arabic term for drum, *tabl*.

Whatever its origins, the earliest pictorial evidence of the tabla in its present shape is to be found in paintings of court life in the 1700s. The tabla player is shown standing with the drums tied around his waist, or sitting down. Women tabla players are occasionally depicted. (See Fig. 3 & 4)

Left: Fig. 4: The Tabla Player is shown standing with the drums tied around her waist.

(Photo credit: Victoria & Albert Museum)

The shapes and sizes of the drums that make the tabla pair have varied quite considerably over the years. Today there are many different tabla-making traditions producing instruments that vary slightly. The tabla described in this manual is typical of those made in the city of Banaras today.

2. The structure of the tabla

The tabla consists of two different drums; the *dahinā* and the *bāyā*. (See Fig. 5)

The dahina (Hindi for 'right') is played with the writing-hand. It is the higher pitched of the two drums and is usually tuned to around C#. A good dahina is made of a very dense, dry piece of wood (*lakaṛī*), that has been chiselled out by hand, leaving a perfectly round mouth. The drum head (*puṛī*) is made of goat skin that is even in thickness and without flaws. The black spot (*syāhī*) forms a perfect circle in the middle of the puri and is approximately one millimetre thick. The leather strap (*baddhī*) laces the puri evenly in place. It is made from buffalo skin and is strong, even in thickness and unbroken. The wooden pegs (*giṭṭak*) are of even thickness and placed at equal intervals around the drum.

The baya (which means 'left') is played with the other hand. It is tuned anywhere from a fourth to an octave below the dahina. A good baya is heavy and made of metal (though one of clay may give a more musical sound). The head is secured to the body with a strong rope (*doṛi*) or goat skin strap (baddhi). If rope is used it is threaded through metal rings (*kaṛī*) at equal intervals. The puri is made of goat skin. The syahi is approximately two millimetres thick and placed off-centre.

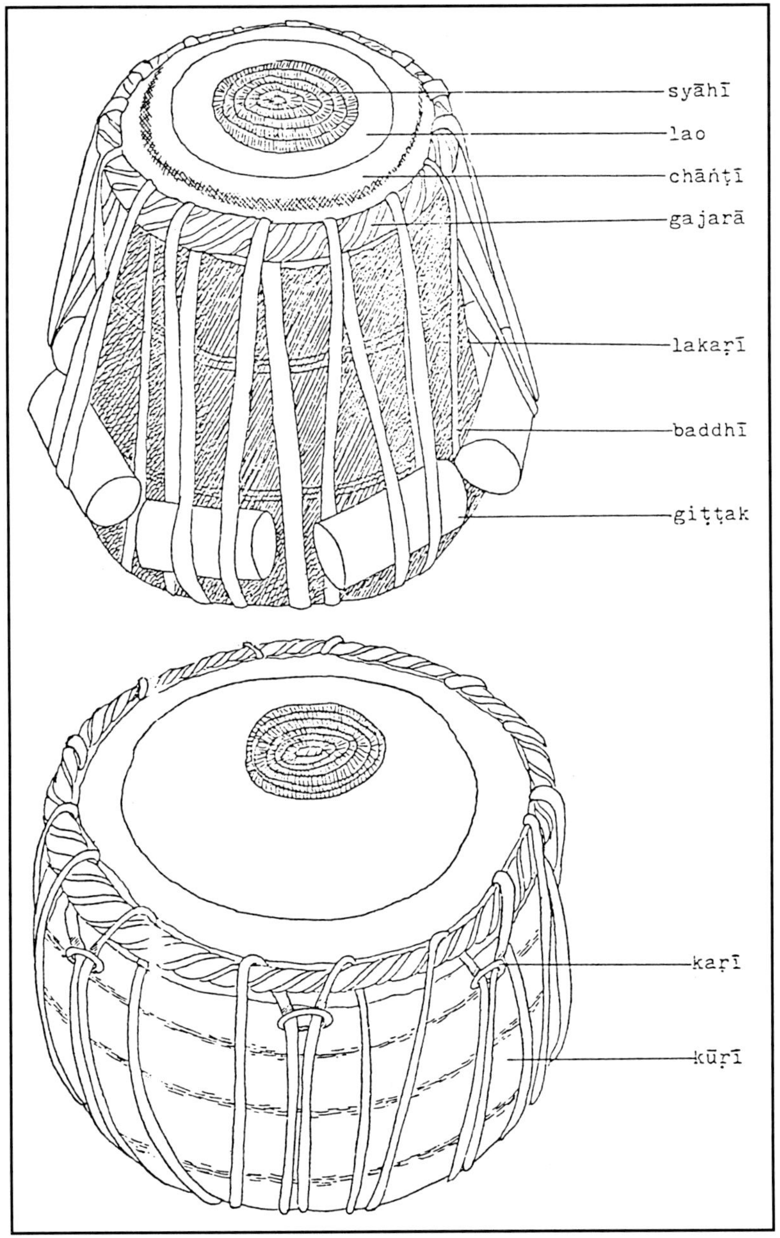

Left: Fig. 5. The tabla consists of two different drums; the dahina and the baya.

3. Caring for your tabla

Like any musical instrument, the tabla should be kept in as even an atmosphere as possible, away from damp and direct heat. Skin becomes taut when dry, and loose when damp. Rope becomes loose when dry, and taut when damp. To lessen the effect of changes, particularly when very humid, protect the puri with cotton-wool padded covers whenever the tabla is not being played (See Fig 6).

The syahi is a semi-permanent paste made from coal dust and iron filings and is finely cracked. It is easily damaged by sharp objects or dissolved by liquids. If it ever becomes wet, do not play the tabla until it has dried thoroughly. In order for the tabla to keep its resonance, both the syahi and the skin of the puri should be kept free of oil and perspiration by applying talcum powder to the hands and puri before playing.

Right: Fig. 6. To lessen the effect of changes, particularly when very humid, protect the puri with cotton-wool padded covers whenever the tabla is not being played.

4. Tuning your tabla

The pitch of the tabla is adjusted by changing the tension of the straps holding the puri in place, or by hitting the *gajarā* of the puri upwards or downwards. There are specially designed hammers (*hathauṛī*) for tuning the tabla. But any small hammer, preferably with a rounded head, will do.

To tune the dahina, begin by adjusting the wooden pegs. They should have the same number of corresponding straps on each of them (and off each of them), and be at the same level. When they are hit down, the pitch of the drum becomes higher. When hit up, the pitch of the drum becomes lower. Do not tune the dahina higher than 'C#' unless it was made to be tuned at a higher pitch.

When the dahina is approximately at the pitch you require, fine tuning is achieved by adjusting the gajara. To fine tune the dahina, the puri is struck using stroke TĀ (see stroke 4 page 14). Beginners may use the following method of striking the puri:-

strike the puri sharply with the right (or left) index finger on the chanti and lao, at a point immediately in front of you. Allow the finger to rebound off so that the puri vibrates freely.

To tune, first strike the puri as above. Rotate the drum with the free hand and hit the puri at various points until you find one that gives the most pleasing and clearest sound. This point is 'A' in Fig. 7.

Tap point 'A' and then rotate the drum so that point 'B' is in the same position that point 'A' was in. Tap point 'B'. If they are not in tune with each other, with the hammer in your other hand tune by:-

1) hitting the gajara downwards at 'B' (if 'B' is lower than 'A')

Below: Fig 7. Diagram of tabla head for tuning.

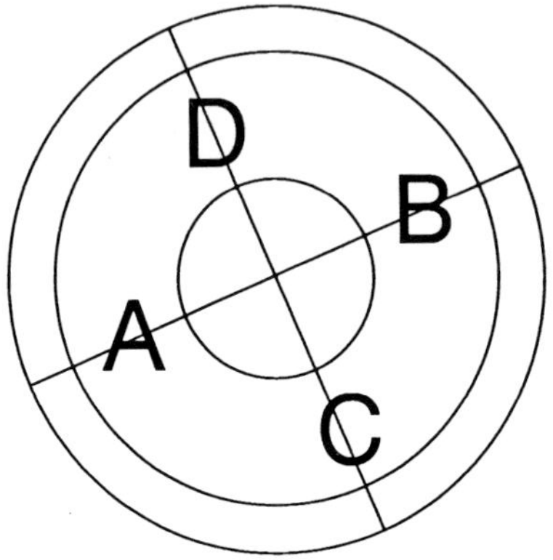

or

2) hitting the gajara upwards at 'B' (if 'B' is higher than 'A')

After each hit with the hammer, strike the puri to ensure that you have not gone beyond the desired pitch. When 'A' and 'B' are in tune with each other, tune 'C' to 'A' in like manner and then 'D' to 'C'.

Check that the four points are in tune and make any final adjustments needed to points 'B', 'C' and 'D' to bring them perfectly in tune with 'A'.

If in tuning you find that any point does not give a clear enough pitch for you to discern whether it may be too high or too low, then tune any other point on the drumhead first.

The baya is tuned with the hammer in a similar manner. However, the metal rings are raised to raise the pitch of the drum and lowered to lower the pitch of the drum. To tune the head perfectly, they may need to be at different levels. If the baya has a leather strap, tuning can be done by placing eight four inch long pieces of half inch thick dowelling under the strap. It can then be tuned like the dahina.

5. Playing the tabla

The tabla is played while sitting on the floor or other firm surface. The drums are placed close together on firm ring-shaped cushions that hold them in place. The dahina is placed at a slight angle forwards (See Fig. 8).

The most popular sitting position for playing the tabla is cross-legged. However, any position that allows you to sit with ease and as close to the drums as possible, can be adopted.

Opposite: Fig. 8. The dahina is placed at a slight angle forwards.

CHAPTER II
Strokes and Notation

1. The strokes of the tabla

The strokes played on the tabla are described by syllables known as *bols*. Each stroke has one or more corresponding bols and a bol may describe a combination of strokes forming a phrase. The bol is an aid to memorising compositions and not a means of notating tabla strokes exactly. Bols can be spoken at great speed and the recitation of compositions is an art practised in itself.

Tabla strokes are executed with the fingers and palm of the hand. Some of the strokes cause the fundamental and harmonics of the tabla head (*puṛī*) to sound and are known as *khulā* (open). Some strokes cause the head to be dampened and are known as *baṅd* (closed).

2. Learning the strokes

The basic strokes of tabla playing are described in this manual with the help of photographs. There are three stages given for each stroke. The first is the learning position. The shape of the hand and the part of the puri to be struck is given. The second is the way the stroke is executed, with the movement of arm and hand required to achieve the correct sound. The third is the final position of the hand when the stroke is completed.

To learn the strokes correctly, look carefully at the arm, hand and wrist positions in the diagrams. It is only on the baya that a wrist and finger action is used to produce the sound. On the dahina, throughout the execution of any stroke, the wrist is kept firm. The fingers alone are not used to execute the strokes. For some dahina strokes you will be required to position the hand by adjusting the angle of the wrist, and never by flicking the wrist.

To play the tabla your hands must be firm, but nevertheless as relaxed as possible without allowing the hand or arm to flop. The thumb and little fingers should be at the same level as the hand. See Fig. 9. This is important if you are to make the best sounds on the tabla and eventually play very quickly. Playing the tabla should not hurt the hand. If it does hurt when you strike the drum, it means that your hand is tense.

NOTE Keep your finger nails trim, as long fingernails will damage the puri.

3. How to play the main strokes

Seven tabla strokes are introduced in this section. Five of them are to be played on the dahina and two on the baya. Each stroke has been given a number or sign and may have more than one bol. Bols are marked with the appropriate diacritics to indicate how they are usually pronounced. A guide to the use of diacritics in this manual is given in the glossary.

Right: Fig 9. The thumb and little fingers should be at the same level as the hand.

DAHINA
Khulla Bol: TUN
Stroke No: 1

THIS STROKE is useful for practising the main position of the hand and arm with the correct degree of firmness. It should be practised on the dahina as described below, as well as with both hands alternately on the baya.

☐ **Learning position of hand:** See Fig. 10a.
Place the hand on the drum with the base of the knuckles on the rim, and with your fingers in the air at an angle of twenty five degrees.

The forearm, wrist and hand should form a straight line from the elbow which is held a little away from the body. See Fig. 10a.

Left: Fig. 10a

Right: Fig. 10b

☐ **Executing the stroke:** See Fig. 10b
Raise your arm keeping the same hand position, firm but not tense. Let the hand fall onto the drum head, the base of the knuckles coming to rest on the rim of the drum.

If you are sufficiently relaxed, the fingers will strike the black spot and rebound off it immediately, making the desired sound.

☐ **Final position of hand:**
Let the hand remain on the drum head, firm and in the learning position.

- **Learning position of hand:** See Fig. 11a
  Place the heel of the hand in the middle of the widest part of the skin of the baya head.

  Allow the wrist to rest on the drumhead.

  Hold the palm and fingers up and at a forty-five degree angle in the air.
- **Executing the stroke:**
  Strike the baya head with the palm of the hand. Do not let the hand rebound off the drumhead.
- **Final position of hand:** See Fig. 11b.
  Keep the hand on the drumhead so that the sound is dampened.

Baya
Band Bol: KI, KĪ or KE
Stroke Sign: —

Right: Fig. 11a

Opposite: Fig. 11b

☐ **Learning position of hand:** See Fig. 12a.
Place the heel of your hand on the lao just behind the syahi. Cup your hand with the knuckles and fingers held high in the air. The forearm, wrist and hand should form a straight line from the elbow, which is held a little away from the body.

☐ **Executing the stroke:** See Fig. 12b
Strike the skin of the drumhead on the lao with the tip of the fingers. The palm of the hand moves a little forward only, while the heel of the hand stays in the same position.

BAYA
Khulla Bol : GHĪ, GHE, GĪ, GE or GA
Stroke Sign: ^

Below left: Fig. 12a

Below right: Fig. 12b

Opposite: Fig. 12c

☐ **Final position of hand:** See Fig. 12c
On contact with the drumhead allow the fingers to rebound off it. Keep the fingers firm, so that they do not bend when they strike the drum head.

Now repeat this stroke, moving all the fingers in the same way, and with the minimum of adjustment, so that at first only the middle finger comes in contact with the drum head, and then only the index finger comes in contact with it.

DAHINA
Band Bol: TE
Stroke No.: 2

☐ **Learning position of hand:** See Fig. 13

Place the hand at a slight angle inwards on the drum, with the whole of the middle and ring fingers resting on the drumhead. Make sure the tips of the fingers are exactly in the centre of the syahi.

☐ **Performing the stroke:** See Fig. 13b

Raise your forearm up into the air. Let it drop while rotating the outer edge of the forearm downwards, and strike the centre of the syahi with the two fingers.

Left: Fig. 13a

Right: Fig. 13b

☐ **Final position of hand:**

Let the hand remain on the drum head in the learning position, so dampening the stroke.

DAHINA
Band Bol: TE
Stroke No.: 3

☐ **Learning position of hand:** See Fig. 14a

Place the hand at a slight angle outwards on the drum, with the whole of the index finger resting on the drum head. Make sure that the tip of the finger is exactly on the centre of the black spot.

☐ **Executing the stroke:** See Fig. 14b

Raise your arm vertically up into the air. Let it drop while rotating the inner edge of the forearm downward, and strike the centre of the syahi with the finger.

Left: Fig. 14a

Right: Fig. 14b

☐ **Final position of the hand:**

Let the hand remain on the drum head in the learning position, so dampening the stroke.

NOTE When playing the strokes TE and ṬE (2 & 3) always keep a space between the index and middle fingers.

DAHINA
Khulla Bol : TĀ or NĀ
Stroke No.: 4

Right: Fig. 15b

Opposite: Fig. 15a

THIS STROKE is used to tune the tabla. It produces the fundamental of the drum head by causing the head to vibrate while being partially dampened. In order to hear the sound you will be aiming to produce with this stroke, place the tip of the index finger of your left hand on the edge of the syahi (furthest away from you) and use the right hand TUN stroke to strike the drum.

With the stroke NĀ you learn to make this sound with the right hand only.

- ☐ **Learning position of hand:** See Fig. 15a

  Position the hand as for playing TUN with the index finger above the lao and the middle finger above the middle of the syahi. Curl the ring finger back until the tip of it rests on the edge of the syahi with the little finger on the chanti. Keep the index and middle fingers as straight as possible and the whole hand firmly in this position but without tension

- ☐ **Executing the stroke:** See Fig. 15b.

  Raise the arm keeping the hand position firm. Let the hand fall onto the drumhead with the base of the knuckles as close to the rim as possible and the tip of the index finger on the edge of the syahi.

  Of their own accord the index finger will strike the lao and the middle finger the syahi, and both fingers will rebound immediately. In executing this stroke the index and middle fingers will feel exactly the same as in TUN.

- ☐ **Final position of hand:**

  Let the hand remain on the head firmly and in the learning position.

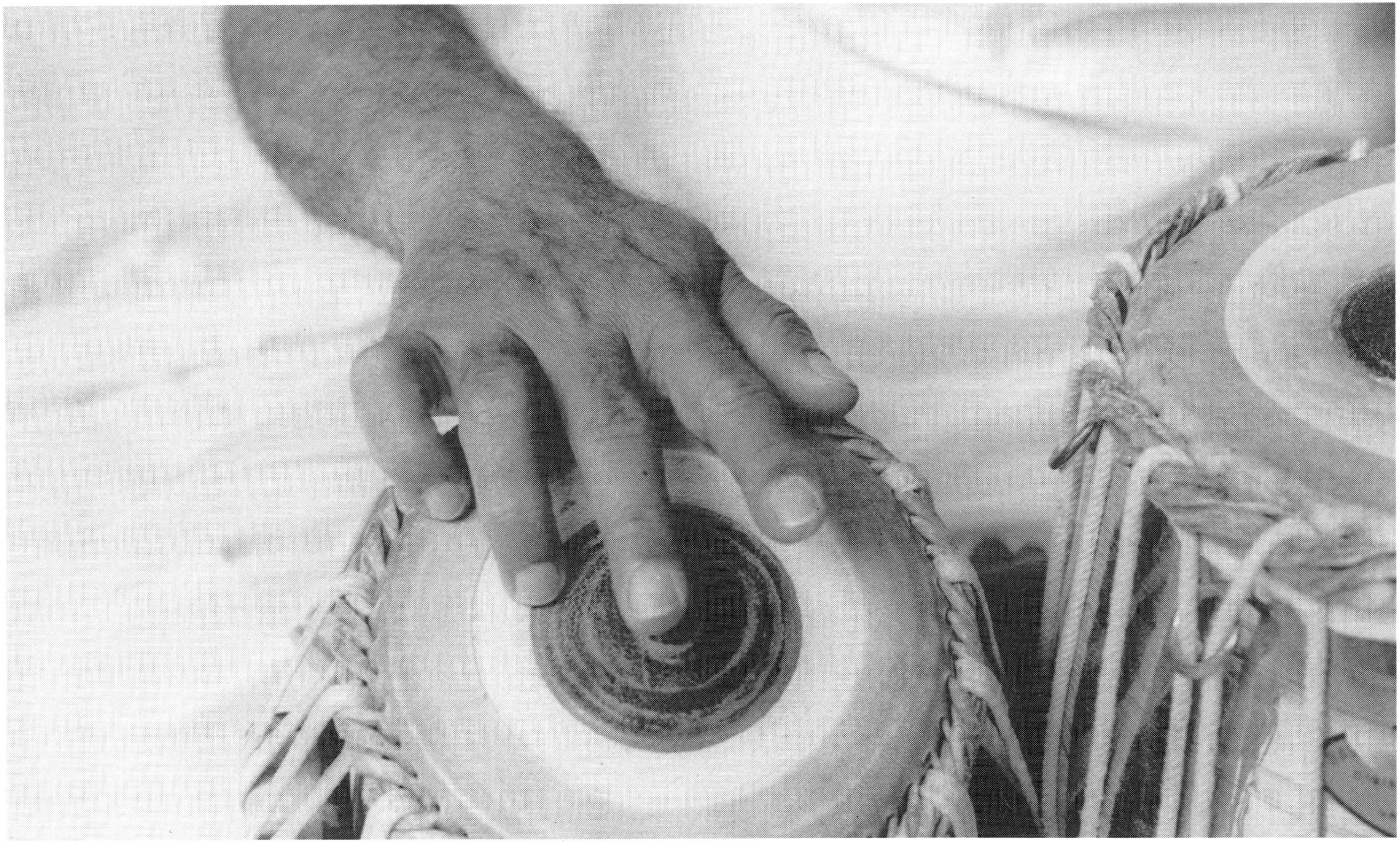

DAHINA
Khulla Bol: TIN
Stroke No.: 5

THIS STROKE is similar to TUN except that only the index finger strikes the drum head.

☐ **Learning position of hand:** See Fig. 16a.

Place the hand on the drum head with only the base of the index finger resting on the rim of the drum head, and all the fingers in the air — the tip of the index finger being held directly above the middle of the black spot.

☐ **Executing the stroke:** See Fig. 16b.

Raise your arm, keeping the hand firm, and let it drop on to the drum head while rotating the inner edge of the forearm downwards. The base of the index finger should come to rest on the rim of the drumhead.

The whole of the index finger will strike the drum head (the tip of the finger coming in contact with the middle of the black spot) and immediately rebound.

☐ **Final position of hand:**

Let the hand remain on the drum head firmly and in its initial position.

Left: Fig. 16a

Right: Fig. 16b

4. Notation

There are two main notation systems (*padati*) in India. One was created by Pandit Vishnudigambar Paluskar and the other by Pandit Vishnu Narayan Bhatkhande. The latter is most widely used because it is simple and easy to operate. Bhatkande padati is used in this manual. The symbols used in this notation are explained below, and as they are introduced.

kostak (sign for a matra (beat))	‿ or ____
ardh viram (divides matra (beat) equally)	,
avagrah (sign for a rest)	S or –
sam (first matra of tal and shown by clap)	+
khali (matra of tal shown by wave)	0
tali (matras of tal shown by claps and numbered in sequence)	+, 2, 3, 4, etc.
vibhag (segment of tal cycle)	|
avartan (one cycle of tal)	||

To this has been added a number for a dahina stroke and a sign for a baya stroke, to enable each to be readily identified. When a new composition is introduced, the bols have their numbers and signs placed beneath them.

CHAPTER III
Kayada and Riaz

1. *Kayada*

The first composition a student learns is *kāyadā*. Kayada is a theme and variation form. The theme is usually an old composition and is itself referred to as the kayada. A kayada is divided into two parts of equal length. The first half is called *khulī* and the second half *muṅdī*.

The following kayada is used to teach beginners the basic strokes on the tabla. Memorise the bols of the khuli of this kayada and then learn to play them on the tabla slowly.

NOTE The bol TI RA is played in the same way as TE ṬE. TI,RA is one beat in length and the same length as KI,ṬA. The beat is divided into two equal parts by the comma (*ardh virām*). TE is also one beat in length. Beats are called *mātrās*.

Khuli of kayada 1 :

BOL:	GHĪ	GHĪ	TE	ṬE	GHĪ	GHĪ	TI,RA	KI,ṬA
dahina:			2	3			2 3	2
baya:	^	^			^	^		-

The second half, the mundi, has the same strokes in the right hand. The left hand strokes differ in the first half of the mundi, the baya stroke GHE is not played. In the second half of the mundi, GHE is played as in the khuli.

Mundi of Kayada 1:

BOL:	KĪ	KĪ	TE	ṬE	GHĪ	GHĪ	TI,RA	KI,ṬA
dahina:			2	3			2 3	2
baya:	-	-			^	^		-

Memorise the bols of the mundi and learn to play them on the tabla. Put together the khuli and mundi to form the complete kayada. Note that the kayada is sixteen matras long.

Kayada 1.

BOL:	GHĪ	GHĪ	TE	ṬE	GHĪ	GHĪ	TI,RA	KI,ṬA
matra:	1	2	3	4	5	6	7	8
BOL:	KĪ	KĪ	TE	ṬE	GHĪ	GHĪ	TI,RA	KI,ṬA
matra:	9	10	11	12	13	14	15	16

Practise this kayada until you can play it several times from memory without a break. Check that you are playing each stroke evenly, with the help of a metronome or tape recorder.

2. *Thah-Dun*

An important convention in tabla playing is to play a composition *ṭhāh-dūn* i.e. to play a composition twice, the second time at double the speed.

The initial tempo, which can be at any speed, is called *ṭhah* and exactly double that speed is called *dūn*. Dun is usually the fastest speed you can play a particular piece. Here is kayada 1 in thah and dun.

Thah:

BOL:	GHĪ	GHĪ	TE	ṬE	GHĪ	GHĪ	TI,RA	KI,ṬA
matra:	1	2	3	4	5	6	7	8
BOL:	KĪ	KĪ	TE	ṬE	GHĪ	GHĪ	TI,RA	KI,ṬA
matra:	9	10	11	12	13	14	15	16

Dun:

BOL:	GHĪ,GHĪ	TE,ṬE	GHĪ,GHĪ	TIRA, KIṬA
matra:	1	2	3	4
BOL:	KĪ,KĪ	TE,ṬE	GHĪ,GHĪ	TIRA,KIṬA
matra:	5	6	7	8

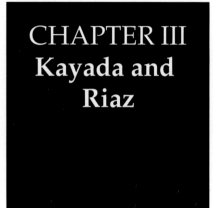

Each underline represents one matra (beat) in length. All the bols in one matra are equal in length. When kayada 1 is played thah it is 16 matras long, and when played dun, 8 matras long.

Practise playing thah-dun until you can change tempo with ease. Use a tape recorder or a metronome and check that you do exactly double the tempo (and halve it) each time.

3. Playing strokes simultaneously

Many tabla bols require you to play a dahina and baya stroke simultaneously. Whenever GHE is played with a dahina stroke, a new bol is formed which begins with the aspirated 'dh'. Here are three such bols:

Khula				
	Bol:	DHĀ	DHIN	DHE
	Dahina:	4	5	3
	Baya:	^	^	^

Practise playing these bols, ensuring that each stroke is accurately executed even though they are being played together.

DHĀ (see fig. 17) is introduced in kayada 2. This is one of the important practice kayadas of professional tabla players. The mundi has the same strokes in the right hand as the khuli. The left hand strokes differ. In the first half of the mundi, the baya stroke GHE is not played. In the second half of the mundi, GHE is played as in the khuli, with an extra GHE added to the stroke TIN to make DHIN.

Right: Fig. 17a

NOTE the baya stroke KĪ is added to the TIN in the khuli.

Kayada 2

khuli	Bol:	DHĀ	DHĀ	TE	ṬE
	D:	4	4	2	3
	B:	^	^		
	Bol:	DHĀ	DHĀ	TIN	NĀ
	D:	4	4	5	4
	B:	^	^	-	
mundi	Bol:	TĀ	TĀ	TE	ṬE
	D:	4	4	2	3
	Bol:	DHĀ	DHĀ	DHIN	NĀ
	D:	4	4	5	4
	B:	^	^	^	

All the strokes of this composition are equal in length and each one matra in length. Practise this kayada until you can play it several times from memory without a break. Check that you are playing each stroke evenly, with the help of a metronome or tape recorder.

Now practise this kayada thah and dun:-

Thah:-

BOL:	DHĀ	DHĀ	TE	TE	DHĀ	DHĀ	TIN	NĀ
matra:	1	2	3	4	5	6	7	8
BOL:	TĀ	TĀ	TE	ṬE	DHĀ	DHĀ	DHIN	NĀ
matra:	9	10	11	12	13	14	15	16

Dun:-

BOL:	DHĀ,DHĀ	TE,ṬE	DHĀ,DHĀ	TIN,NĀ
matra:	1	2	3	4
BOL:	TĀ,TĀ	TE,ṬE	DHĀ,DHĀ	DHIN,NĀ
matra:	5	6	7	8

NOTE that this kayada is sixteen matras long when played thah, and eight matras long when played dun.

4. *Kayada 3*

Like kayada 2, this is an important practice kayada. TI,RA is one matra in length and is equal in time to KI,ṬA, DHĀ, etc.

Learn to play, memorise and practise this kayada.

Kayada 3

khuli	Bol:	DHĀ	DHĀ	TI,RA	KI,ṬA
	D:	4	4	2 3	2
	B:	^	^		-
	Bol:	DHĀ	DHĀ	TIN	NĀ
	D:	4	4	5	4
	B:	^	^	-	
mundi	Bol:	TĀ	TĀ	TI,RA	KI,ṬA
	D:	4	4	2 3	2
	B:				-
	Bol	DHĀ	DHĀ	DHIN	NĀ
	D:	4	4	5	4
	B:	^	^	^	

Opposite: Fig. 17b

5. *Riaz*

Riaz is more than its literal meaning, 'practice', implies. It is a highly skilled discipline requiring great willpower, concentration and stamina. It can be said to be the ability to surrender oneself to one's art, and even a kind of meditation.

Tabla players train for long hours over many years to achieve the proficiency, dexterity and clarity required in the performance of their instrument, and to attain speeds of over twenty individual strokes per second. Much of the tabla repertoire was conceived at such speeds, and many compositions are rendered meaningless and lose their beauty, when performed at slower speeds.

Greatness as a tabla player seems to be synonymous with extraordinary devotion to practising. Stories are told of the tremendous sacrifices made by tabla players in order to master their instrument. It is not unusual to hear of an artist who has practised twelve hours a day for two years (with the minimum of breaks to eat and sleep) early on in his career. To do this the artist would have given up his only source of income, that of concerts, and he and his family would have had to live austerely.

So be quite prepared to have your progress and potential as a tabla player judged by the amount of riaz you do.

At the end of this chapter, and subsequent chapters, you will find practice schedules based on what you have learnt. Choose your practice schedule according to the minimum time you will have available every day. Systematic and regular practice is more valuable than the occasional long practice session. Use any extra time you may have to go over other material.

As your repertoire grows, modify your practice schedule to include new pieces that you have memorised. If your time for practising is limited, alternate the pieces in your schedule weekly.

One of the aims of riaz is to improve your ability to concentrate, and to think and plan ahead. It is important that you follow your chosen practice schedule meticulously, and that you do not stop playing for the duration of the practice. If your hands do become tired, slow down by playing at half or even quarter the original tempo.

Another aim of riaz is to improve your technique. While practising at the thah tempo, try to perfect your technique by adjusting your hand and arm positions and ensuring that your shoulders, arms and fingers are free of tension. When you increase the tempo try to maintain the level of your technique.

In order to get the best results from your practice you must memorise the pieces and their sequence. The repetitive element of riaz will help with this. However it is advisable to spend some time away from the tabla memorising the pieces and familiarising yourself with the technique for playing the strokes.

□ RIAZ SCHEDULE

30 minutes daily

6 minutes	Kayada 1 — thah
4 minutes	Kayada 1 — dun
5 minutes	Kayada 2 — thah
5 minutes	Kayada 2 — dun
5 minutes	Kayada 3 — thah
5 minutes	Kayada 3 — dun

CHAPTER IV
Palta and Laya

1. Improvisation

An important part of training to be a tabla player is learning how to improvise. Improvisation takes many different forms in a tabla player's repertoire. In this manual you will be introduced to the elementary principles of three of the most important types of improvisation. The first is how to develop a kayada in performance by improvising on the kayada theme with paltas and pench. The second is how to construct a cadential phrase called the tihai that is improvised within a precise mathematical framework. And the third is how to elaborate the bols of the theka with kisme, while still keeping the main characteristics of the tal. Paltas and pench are introduced in this chapter, kisme and tihai in chapter V.

2. Palta and pench

Palṭā is a variation on a kayada which uses the same bols as the kayada. Paltas have the same khuli-mundi form as kayada. They can be played at any speed.

There are two ways of making a palta. The most popular way, *pench,* is made by repeating the bols of a kayada in various ways. A pench is twice as long as its kayada. Here are four pench on kayada 1 with both khuli and mundi written out in double the speed of the kayada i.e. two bols to one matra.

1.	GHI,GHI	TE,TE	GHI,GHI	TE,TE
	GHI,GHI	TE,TE	GHI,GHI	TIRA,KITA
	KI,KI	TE,TE	KI,KI	TE,TE
	GHI,GHI	TE,TE	GHI,GHI	TIRA,KITA
2.	GHI,GHI	TE,TE	TE,TE	TE,TE
	GHI,GHI	TE,TE	GHI,GHI	TIRA,KITA
	KI,KI	TE,TE	TE,TE	TE,TE
	GHI,GHI	TE,TE	GHI,GHI	TIRA,KITA
3.	GHI,GHI	GHI,GHI	TE,TE	TE,TE
	GHI,GHI	TE,TE	GHI,GHI	TIRA,KITA
	KI,KI	KI,KI	TE,TE	TE,TE
	GHI,GHI	TE,TE	GHI,GHI	TIRA,KITA
4.	GHI,GHI	GHI,GHI	GHI,GHI	TE,TE
	GHI,GHI	TE,TE	GHI,GHI	TIRA,KITA
	KI,KI	KI,KI	KI,KI	TE,TE
	GHI,GHI	TE,TE	GHI,GHI	TIRA,KITA

Memorise these pench and practise playing them one after the other without stopping.

The other way of making paltas is by rearranging the bols of a kayada or its pench. These paltas are on the whole more difficult to play than pench.

Here are six paltas on the theme of kayada 1. They are the same length as the kayada although they are twice the speed of the kayada i.e. two bols to one matra.

1.	GHI,TE	TE,GHI	GHI,GHI	TIRA,KITA
	KI,TE	TE,KI	GHI,GHI	TIRA,KITA
2.	TE,TE	GHI,GHI	GHI,GHI	TIRA,KITA
	TE,TE	KI,KI	GHI,GHI	TIRA,KITA
3.	GHI,GHI	GHI,GHI	TE,TE	TIRA,KITA
	KI,KI	KI,KI	TE,TE	TIRA,KITA
4.	TIRA,KITA	GHI,GHI	GHI,GHI	TE,TE
	TIRA,KITA	KI,KI	GHI,GHI	TE,TE
5.	GHI,TIRA	KITA,GHI	GHI,GHI	TE,TE
	KI,TIRA	KITA,KI	GHI,GHI	TE,TE
6.	TIRA,KITA	TE,TE	GHI,GHI	GHI,GHI
	TIRA,KITA	TE,TE	GHI,GHI	GHI,GHI

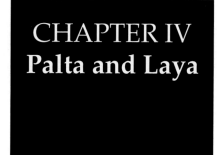

Below are paltas based on pench number 1 of kayada 1. The mundi has been written out for palta number 1 only. In the other paltas the point at which the playing of the baya stroke is resumed in the mundi is indicated by an asterisk (*).

1.	GHI,GHI	TE,TE	GHI,TE	TE,GHI
	GHI,GHI	TE,TE	GHI,GHI	TIRA,KITA
	KI,KI	TE,TE	KI,TE	TE,KI
	GHI,GHI	TE,TE	GHI,GHI	TIRA,KITA
2.	GHI,TE	TE,GHI	GHI,TE	TE,GHI
	*GHI,GHI	TE,TE	GHI,GHI	TIRA,KITA
	mundi			
3.	GHI,GHI	GHI,TE	TE,GHI	GHI,TE
	*TE,GHI	TE,TE	GHI,GHI	TIRA,KITA
	mundi			
4.	TE,TE	GHI,GHI	TE,TE	GHI,GHI
	*GHI,GHI	TE,TE	GHI,GHI	TIRA,KITA
	mundi			
5.	TE,TE	GHI,TE	TE,GHI	GHI,GHI
	*GHI,GHI	TE,TE	GHI,GHI	TIRA,KITA
	mundi			
6.	TE,TE	GHI,GHI	GHI,TE	TE,GHI
	*GHI,GHI	TE,TE	GHI,GHI	TIRA,KITA
	mundi			

Practise playing all the pench followed by the paltas on pench number 1, one after the other without stopping. Also practise the paltas on the kayada theme. See how many paltas and pench you can create on the theme without splitting TEṬE and TIRAKIṬA.

Pench are generally referred to as palta and in performance pench and palta are mixed. Now that you are clear about the difference between them, we will refer to pench as palta also.

3. Paltas for kayada 2

The same process for making paltas is followed.

The mundi of palta number 1 is written out. The mundi of the rest of the paltas follow the same pattern.

1.	DHA,DHA	TE,TE	DHA,DHA	TE,TE
	DHA,DHA	TE,TE	DHA,DHA	TIN,NA
	TA,TA	TE,TE	TA,TA	TE,TE
	DHA,DHA	TE,TE	DHA,DHA	DHIN,NA
2.	DHA,DHA	TE,TE	TE,TE	TE,TE
	*DHA,DHA	TE,TE	DHA,DHA	TIN,NA
	mundi			
3.	DHA,DHA	TE,TE	DHA,TE	TE,DHA
	*DHA,DHA	TE,TE	DHA,DHA	TIN,NA
	mundi			
4.	DHA,TE	TE,DHA	DHA,TE	TE,DHA
	*DHA,DHA	TE,TE	DHA,DHA	TIN,NA
	mundi			
5.	DHA,DHA	DHA,TE	TE,DHA	DHA,TE
	*TE,DHA	TE,TE	DHA,DHA	TIN,NA
	mundi			
6.	DHA,DHA	DHA,DHA	TE,TE	TE,TE
	*DHA,DHA	TE,TE	DHA, DHA	TIN,NA
	mundi			

Memorise these paltas and practise playing them one after the other without stopping.

4. *Kayada 3*

Paltas for kayada 2 can be played for kayada 3 by substituting TIRA KIṬA for TE ṬE. Here is palta 1 for kayada 3.

1.

DHA,DHA	TIRA,KITA	DHA,DHA	TIRA,KITA
DHA,DHA	TIRA,KITA	DHA,DHA	TIN,NA
TA,TA	TIRA,KITA	TA,TA	TIRA,KITA
DHA,DHA	TIRA,KITA	DHA,DHA	DHIN,NA

Write out the other paltas for kayada 3 and memorise them.

5. *Kayada 4.*

The stroke that gives the tabla its distinctive almost metallic ringing sound is called TĀ or NĀ and is played on the chanti. It is similar to stroke 4, also called TĀ or NĀ. In this kayada the chanti TĀ is played. A description of how to play this stroke is given opposite.

Kayada 4

khuli		DHĀ	TI,RA	KI,ṬA	TA,KA
	D:	6	2 3	2	3
	B:	^		-	-
		DHĀ	TI,RA	KI,ṬA	TA,KA
		DHĀ	TI,RA	KI,ṬA	TA,KA
		TIN	NĀ	KI,ṬA	TA,KA
	D:	5	6	2	3
	B:	-		-	-
mundi		TĀ	TI,RA	KI,ṬA	TA,KA
	D:	6	2 3	2	3
	B:			-	-
		TĀ	TI,RA	KI,ṬA	TA,KA
		DHĀ	TI,RA	KI,ṬA	TA,KA
		DHIN	NĀ	KI,ṬA	TA,KA
	D:	5	6	2	3
	B:	^		-	-

NOTE that the new bol TA KA is played exactly as ṬE followed by KI. To change the position of the hand from DHĀ to play TIRA KIṬA, straighten the arm at the wrist.

DAHINA
khulla Bol: NĀ or TĀ
Stroke No.: 6

N.B. This stroke position is very similar to TĀ (stroke number 4).

Left: Fig. 18a

- ☐ **Learning position of hand:** See Fig. 18a.

  Position the hand as for TĀ (4). Extend the arm slightly outwards at the wrist and elbow with the ring finger acting as a pivot until the index finger is above the chanti. The hand will form a slight angle at the wrist.

- ☐ **Executing the stroke:** See Fig. 18b.

  Raise the hand off the drum by rotating the inner arm away from you.

  Rotate the inner arm downwards hitting the chanti with the index finger, without changing the angle of the wrist. Immediately raise the inner arm and inner section of the hand up again. This allows the drum head to vibrate while partially dampened by the ring finger on the edge of the syahi.

- ☐ **Final position of hand:**

  Leave the hand in the air, keeping the index finger on the edge of the syahi as in Fig. 18a.

Left: Fig 18b

Memorise the following paltas for kayada 4.

1. DHA,TIRA KITA,TAKA DHA,TIRA KITA,TAKA
DHA,TIRA KITA,TAKA DHA,TIRA KITA,TAKA
*DHA,TIRA KITA,TAKA DHA,TIRA KITA,TAKA
DHA,TIRA KITA,TAKA TIN,NA KITA,TAKA
mundi

2. DHA,TIRA KITA,TAKA DHA,TIRA KITA,DHA
TIRA,KITA DHA,TIRA KITA,DHA TIRA,KITA
*DHA,TIRA KITA,TAKA DHA,TIRA KITA,TAKA
DHA,TIRA KITA,TAKA TIN,NA KITA,TAKA
mundi

3. DHA,TIRA KITA,DHA TIRA,KITA DHA,TIRA
KITA,DHA TIRA,KITA DHA,TIRA KITA,TAKA
*DHA,TIRA KITA,TAKA DHA,TIRA KITA,TAKA
DHA,TIRA KITA,TAKA TIN,NA KITA,TAKA
mundi

4. DHA,TIRA KITA,DHA TIRA,KITA DHA,TIRA
KITA,TAKA DHA,TIRA KITA,DHA TIRA,KITA
*DHA,TIRA KITA,TAKA DHA,TIRA KITA,TAKA
DHA,TIRA KITA,TAKA TIN,NA KITA,TAKA
mundi

5. DHA,TIRA KITA,DHA TIRA,KITA TAKA,DHA
TIRA,KITA DHA,TIRA KITA,DHA TIRA,KITA
*DHA,TIRA KITA,TAKA DHA,TIRA KITA,TAKA
DHA,TIRA KITA,TAKA TIN,NA KITA,TAKA
mundi

6. Laya and Layakari

There are three *laya* (tempos) normally used in the performance of Indian music. They are *vilambit* (slow), *madhya* (medium) and *drut* (fast). These three tempos do not express precise speeds. They are guides, telling one whether the tal (time cycle) is to be in slow, medium, or fast tempo.

A very important part of tabla playing is the method used for accelerating or reducing the original speed at which a piece is played without changing the laya of the tal it is in. This is done by changing the way in which a matra is divided and is called *layakārī*. You have already learnt to do this in the lesson on thah-dun.

There are many different types of layakari: this manual explains only two — *barābar* and *āṛī*.

When a composition is played at the same speed as the tal, twice as fast as the tal, four times as fast as the tal and eight times as fast as the tal, etc., it is called barabar.

Each of these rhythms of barabar are known as *gun* and each has a separate name.

Here is the khuli of kayada 1 written out in the various guns of barabar layakari.

EKGUN: DHĀ DHĀ TE ṬE DHĀ DHĀ TIN NĀ

In this gun there is one bol to one matra.

As you have already learnt, an underline indicates that all the bols on it are to be played within the duration of one matra, that a comma divides the matra into equal sections, and that all the bols in a matra, or section of a matra, are of equal duration. In the next example, the sign (S) for a rest is used. It is known as an *avagrah* and is equal in duration to a bol in the same matra. The kayada has been notated in the same speed as above.

EKGUN: DHĀ,S DHĀ,S TE,S ṬE,S
DHĀ,S DHĀ,S TIN,S NĀ,S

DUGUN: DHĀ,DHĀ TE,ṬE DHĀ,DHĀ TIN,NĀ

In dugun there are two bols to every matra, hence it is twice as fast as ekgun.

CHAUGUN: DHĀ,DHĀ,TE,ṬE DHĀ,DHĀ,TIN,NĀ

In chaugun the kayada is four times as fast as in ekgun.

ĀṬHGUN: DHĀ,DHĀ,TE,ṬE, DHĀ,DHĀ,TIN,NĀ

Here the matra is divided into eight equal parts and the kayada is played eight times as fast as in ekgun.

Practise reciting these examples, marking time very slowly with claps. Keep the matra (i.e. the duration of your clap) constant throughout, so that only the speed of the bols and hence the kayada is increased.

In *ari* layakari, the speed of a composition is increased in multiples of three. Hence a composition is either one and a half times as fast as the tal, three times as fast as the tal, six times as fast as the tal, twelve times as fast as the tal, etc. Here are the various guns of ari layakari.

ḌEṚHGUN:

DHĀ,S,DHĀ S,TE,S ṬE,S,DHĀ S,DHĀ,S TIN,S,NĀ

In derhgun each matra is divided into three equal parts — these equal divisions being shown by the commas, and there are three bols for every two matras.

TIGUN: DHĀ,DHĀ,TE ṬE,DHĀ,DHĀ TIN,NĀ,etc.

Here the kayada is three times as fast as in ekgun and twice as fast as in derhgun.

The kayada should be repeated until the final bol comes at the end of a matra.

Say the kayada with claps at this speed and see how many times it has to be repeated in order to end at the end of a matra.

CHHAGUN: DHĀ,DHĀ,TE,ṬE,DHĀ,DHĀ TIN,NĀ,etc.

Here the kayada is twice as fast as tigun and, as with tigun, the kayada has to be repeated several times for its final bol to come at the end of a matra.

Practise changing from barabar to ari layakaris with reciting the various guns. Use a metronome or a tape recorder to check that you do not change the duration of the matra with the gun.

Also practise saying the other kayadas you know in this way.

Note that TIRA is equal to one matra in ekgun thus:

EKGUN:

DHĀ DHĀ TIRA KIṬA DHĀ DHĀ TIN NĀ

DERHGUN:

DHĀ,S,DHĀ S,TI,RA KI,ṬA,DHĀ S,DHĀ,S
TIN,S,NĀ S,TĀ,S TĀ,S,TI RA,KI,ṬA etc.

7. *Kayada 5*

So far, all the kayadas you have learnt have been in barabar layakari. There are many kayadas composed in other layakaris. Here is a kayada in derhgun which is in ari layakari.

Kayada 5. LAYAKARI - ARI

Tali:	+			
Matra:	1	2	3	4
Bol:	DHĀ S TI	RA KI ṬA	DHĀ S GHE	S NĀ S
D:	6 2	3 2	6	6
B:	^	-	^ ^	

Tali:	2			
Matra:	5	6	7	8
Bol:	DHĀ S GHE	S TI S	NĀ S KI	S NĀ S
D:	6	5	6	6
B:	^ ^	-	-	

Tali:	0			
Matra:	9	10	11	12
Bol:	TĀ S TI	RA KI ṬA	DHĀ S GHE	S NĀ S
D:	6 2	3 2	6	6
B:		-	^ ^	

Tali:	3			
Matra:	13	14	15	16
Bol:	DHĀ S GHE	S DHI S	NĀ S GHI	S NĀ S
D:	6	5	6	6
B:	^ ^	^	^	

All the strokes of this kayada are known to you. Memorise this kayada and practise playing it thah-dun. The dun of derhgun is tigun. Here is kayada 5, written in tigun.

Kayada 5 LAYAKARI - ARI

Tali:	+			
Matra:	1	2	3	4
BOL:	DHĀ,TIRA,KIṬA	DHĀ,GHE,NĀ	DHĀ,GHE,TI	NĀ,KI,NĀ
Tali:	2			
Matra:	5	6	7	8
BOL:	TĀ,TIRA,KIṬA	DHĀ,GHE,NĀ	DHĀ,GHE,DHI	NĀ,GHI,NĀ

The paltas of a kayada are normally played at the same speed as the kayada it follows. Here are paltas for kayada 5. They are in tigun.

1.	DHA,TIRA,KITA	DHA,GHE,NA	DHA,TIRA,KITA	DHA,GHE,NA
	*DHA,TIRA,KITA	DHA,GHE,NA	DHA,GHE,TI	NA,KI,NA
	mundi			
2.	DHA,TIRA,KITA	DHA,TIRA,KITA	DHA,TIRA,KITA	DHA,GHE,NA
	*DHA,TIRA,KITA	DHA,GHE,NA	DHA,GHE,TI	NA,KI,NA
	mundi			
3.	DHA,TIRA, KITA	TIRA, KITA,DHA	DHA,TIRA,KITA	DHA,GHE,NA
	*DHA,TIRA,KITA	DHA,GHE,NA	DHA,GHE,TI	NA,KI,NA
	mundi			
4.	DHA,TIRA,KITA	TIRA,KITA,DHA	TIRA,KITA,DHA	TIRA,KITA,DHA
	*DHA,TIRA,KITA	DHA,GHE,NA	DHA,GHE,TI	NA,KI,NA
	mundi			
5.	DHA,GHE,NA	DHA,TIRA,KITA	DHA,TIRA,KITA	DHA,GHE,NA
	*DHA,TIRA,KITA	DHA,GHE,NA	DHA,GHE,TI	NA,KI,NA
	mundi			

8. Riaz Schedules

Here are two schedules for daily practice, one for 30 and one for 60 minutes. These can be lengthened by increasing the time spent on each stage of the practice. Every kayada is first to be played thah, then dun, dun being the fastest speed at which you can play the kayada properly. This dun speed will increase as your playing improves. Try to practise without breaking in the middle of a piece or between sections. Check your fingering, make sure your speed is constant within a section and that every stroke is evenly spaced.

☐ 30 MINUTES DAILY

6 mins. Kayada 2 — thah
4 mins. Kayada 2 — dun:
6 mins. Paltas of kayada 2
Play each palta several times. If you are unable to play them at the same speed you played the kayada dun, choose a slightly slower tempo.
4 mins. Kayada 3 — thah.
Try to keep the duration of the matra (tempo) the same as for the paltas of kayada 2.
4 mins. Kayada 3 — dun
6 mins. Paltas of kayada 3.
(To be practised as paltas of kayada 2.)

☐ 60 MINUTES DAILY

3 mins. Kayada 2 thah.
5 mins. Kayada 2 dun.
10 mins. Paltas kayada 2.
3 mins. Kayada 3 thah.
3 mins. Kayada 3 dun.
8 mins. Paltas kayada 3.
4 mins. Kayada 4 dun.
10 mins. Paltas of kayada 4.
6 mins. Kayada 5 tigun
8 mins. Paltas of kayada 5

1. *Tal*

Tāl is the time-measure of Indian music. There are over 300 tals. Some tals are only used in classical music and others only for light and folk music.

A tal is counted in cycles of stresses of varying intensities. Each tal has its own characteristic arrangement of stresses. Here is the time cycle tīntāl. It is the most popular tal in classical music. The kayadas you have learnt so far are in this tal. One cycle (*āvartan*) of tintal is sixteen matras long. And the matras are grouped into four sections (*vibhāg*) each consisting of four matras. (See diagram below right)

Every matra is a stress point. The first matra is called *sam* and is marked with a plus sign. It is the point of greatest stress. The next two matras with stresses of lesser intensity, called *tālī*, are marked with a 2 and a 3. All other matras (except 9) are stresses of even lighter intensity. Matra 9, which is marked with 0, is the stress of least intensity. It is called *khālī*.

There is a way of signing a tal that uses claps, waves and fingers, and the arrangement of these for any given tal is referred to as the *tālī* of that tal.

The signing for tintal is written out below.

Tali	+	2	0	3	+	
Matras	1 2 3 4	5 6 7 8	9 10 11 12	13 14 15 16	1	etc.
Sign	clap	clap	wave	clap	clap	

It is useful to be able to give the tali for tintal accurately so that you can keep time for musicians while they are performing. Practise saying tintal with claps at different laya (tempos), starting as slowly as possible and ending up as quickly as possible. To say tintal really quickly, do only the clapping and waves without counting, like this:-

CHAPTER V
Tal and Tihai

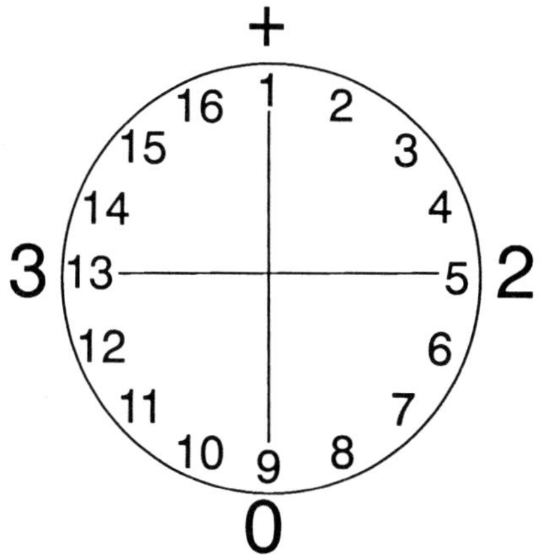

Tintal - drut laya

tali:	+	2	0	3	
matra:	1	5	9	13	(recite)
sign:	clap	clap	wave	clap	

There are many different ways of showing the tali. The following is one way of counting the matras of the tal to enable you to check that you are playing a piece correctly.

The matras, 2, 3 and 4 are shown by pressing the ring finger, middle finger and index finger (in that order) of the right hand, into the palm of the left hand. Matras 6, 7, and 8, and, 14, 15 and 16 are counted in this way also. Matras 10, 11 and 12 are counted by pressing these same fingers against the thumb of the right hand.

Memorise counting tintal in this way until you can do it without thinking.

2. Theka

Tals are also known by the way they are played on the tabla. Each tal has its own peculiar arrangement of bols. This is known as *ṭhekā*. The theka does not always reinforce the cycle of stresses of the tal but may go against it as in the theka for tintal. The theka for tintal is often referred to as 'NĀ DIN DIN NĀ'.

TĪNTĀL ṬHEKĀ

Tali:	+				2			
Matra:	1	2	3	4	5	6	7	8
Theka:	DHĀ	DHIN	DHIN	DHĀ	DHĀ	DHIN	DHIN	DHĀ
D:	6	4	4	6	6	4	4	6
B:	^	^	^	^	^	^	^	^

Tali:	0				3			
Matra:	9	10	11	12	13	14	15	16
Theka:	DHĀ	TIN	TIN	TĀ	TĀ	DHIN	DHIN	DHĀ
D:	6	4	4	6	6	4	4	6
B:	^	–	–			^	^	^

All the strokes of this theka are known to you. Learn to play the bols NĀ (6) and TIN (4) in the way described on pages 32 to 35 before playing this theka. There is a slight variation in the way of executing them that will enable you to play the theka of tintal quickly and accurately.

When playing this theka ensure that you adjust your wrist minutely between the strokes TĀ (6) and TIN (4) and perform each correctly and accurately.

DAHINA
Khulla Bol: NA or TA
Stroke No.: 6

Below: Fig. 19a

Opposite: Fig. 19b

- ☐ **Learning position of hand:** See Fig. 18a.
  As described on page 26.
- ☐ **Executing the stroke:** See Fig. 19a.
  Raise the hand off the drum by rotating the inner arm away from you with the tip of the index finger remaining in position on the edge of the syahi.

  Rotate the inner arm downwards hitting the chanti with the index finger, and immediately raise the inner arm and inner section of the hand up again.
- ☐ **Final position of hand:** See Fig. 19b.
  As described on page 26.

NOTE that the wrist is at a slight angle during the execution of this stroke.

- ☐ **Learning position of hand:** See Fig. 15a.
  As described on page 14.
- ☐ **Executing the stroke:** See Fig. 20a.
  Raise the arm keeping the tip of the ring finger on the edge of the syahi.

  Let the hand fall on to the drum head with the base of the knuckles as close as possible to the rim of the drum.
- ☐ **Final position of hand:** See Fig. 20b.
  As described on page 14.

NOTE that the wrist is straight and in line with the forearm and hand when executing this stroke.

Right: Fig. 20a

Opposite: Fig. 20b

DAHINA
Khulla Bol: NA, TA or TIN
Stroke No.: 4

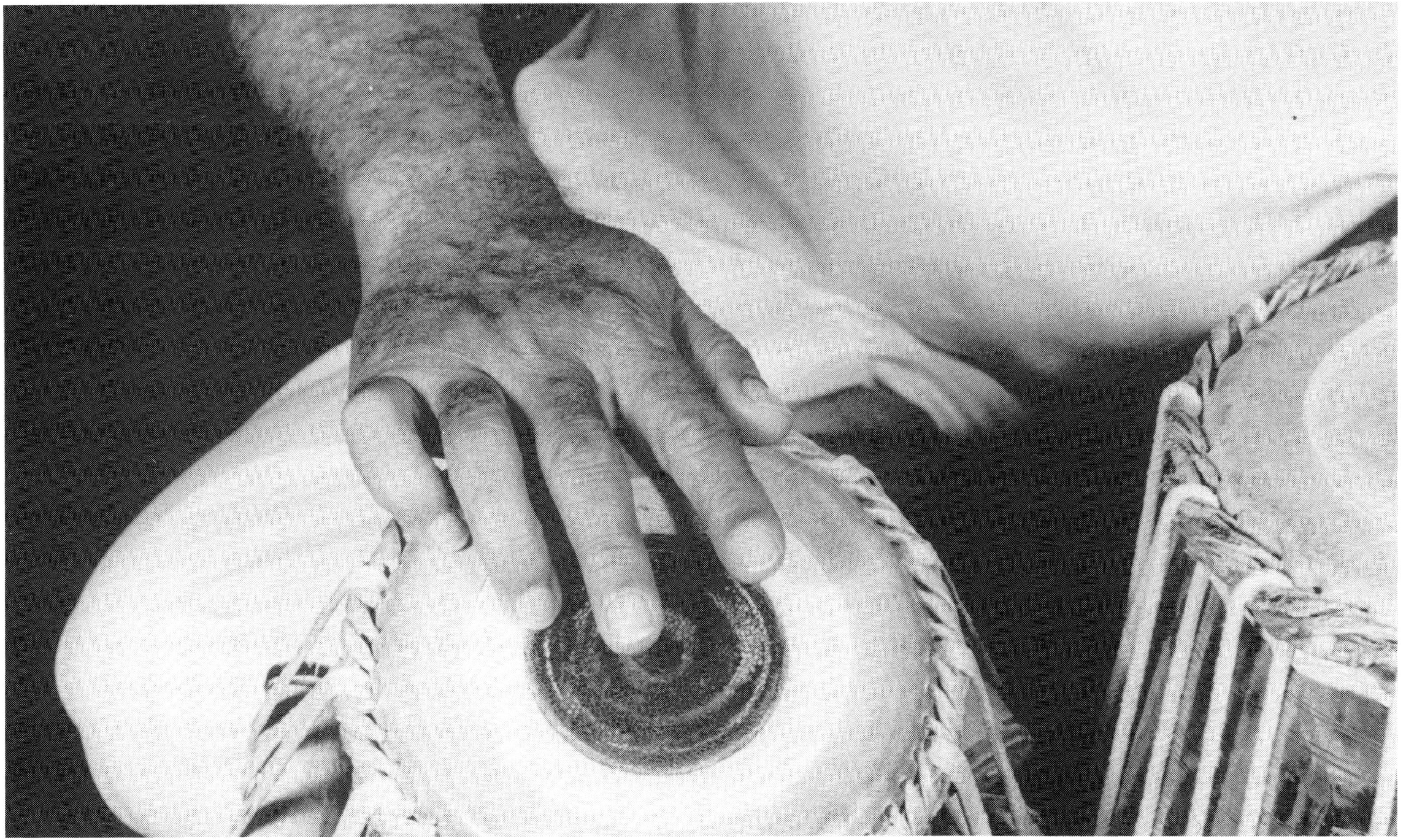

3. *Kisme*

Another improvised form of tabla playing is *kisme.* It is the elaboration on the theka of a tal, while keeping recognisable the characteristics of that tal. The tempo of the tal is either vilambit or madhya, and the decorating bol phrases subdivide the matra.

Here are several examples of kisme which give some of the bol phrases commonly used when performing tintal. Memorise and practise them.

REMEMBER that the comma divides the matra into two sections of equal duration, and that in each section the bols are of equal length.

1. +

DHĀ DHIN DHIN,DHIN DHĀ / (2) DHĀ DHIN DHIN, DHIN DHĀ /

0

DHĀ TIN TIN,TIN TĀ / (3) TĀ DHIN DHIN,DHIN DHĀ//

2. +

DHĀ GHE DHIN DHIN,DHIN DHĀ /

2

DHĀ GHE DHIN DHIN,DHIN DHĀ /

0

DHĀ GHE TIN TIN,TIN TĀ /

3

TĀ KE DHIN DHIN,DHIN DHĀ //

3. +

DHĀ GHE,TIRA KIṬA DHIN DHIN,DHIN DHĀ /

2

DHĀ GHE TIRA KIṬA DHIN DHIN,DHIN DHĀ /

0

DHĀ GHE,TIRA KIṬA TIN TIN,TIN TĀ/

3

TĀ KE,TIRA KIṬA DHIN DHIN,DHIN DHĀ /

4. In this kisme TIT is stroke number 2.

+

DHĀ GHE,TIRA KIṬA DHIN DHIN,DHIN DHĀ,TIT /

2

DHĀ GHE,TIRA KIṬA DHIN DHIN,DHIN DHĀ,TIT /

0

DHĀ GHE,TIRA KIṬA TIN TIN,TIN TĀ,TIT /

3

TĀ KE,TIRA KIṬA DHIN DHIN,DHIN DHĀ,TIT //

Rest (avagrah) have been introduced into the following examples of kisme. Count carefully to ensure that each matra is divided equally and that rests and bols are given their correct time value.

5. In this kisme TIT and TA (not TĀ) are stroke number 2.

+

DHĀ GHE,TIRA KIṬA DHIN S,S TA DHIN,DHIN DHĀ,TIT /

2

DHĀ GHE,TIRA KIṬA DHIN S,S TA DHIN,DHIN DHĀ,TIT /

0

DHĀ GHE,TIRA KIṬA TIN S,S TA TIN,TIN TĀ,TIT /

3

TĀ KE,TIRA KIṬA DHIN S,S TA DHIN,DHIN DHĀ,TIT //

6. The single TE at the end of each line is stroke number 2.

6. +

DHĀ GHE,TE ṬE DHIN DHIN,DHIN S DHĀ,DHĀ TE /

2

DHĀ GHE,TE ṬE DHIN DHIN,DHIN S DHĀ,DHĀ TE /

0

DHĀ GHE,TE ṬE TIN TIN,TIN S TĀ,TĀ TE /

3

TĀ KE,TE ṬE DHIN DHIN,DHIN S DHĀ,DHĀ TE //

The decorating bol phrases can be played in any order. The following examples will give you some idea of how kisme is played.

1. +
DHĀ GHE,TE ṬE DHIN DHIN,DHIN DHĀ,TE /
2
DHĀ GHE,TIRA KIṬA DHIN DHIN,DHIN DHĀ /
0
DHĀ,GHE TIN TIN TIN TĀ TE /
3
TĀ KE,TE ṬE DHIN DHIN,DHIN S DHĀ,DHĀ TIT //

2. +
DHĀ DHIN DHIN,DHIN DHĀ /
2
DHĀ,GHE DHIN DHIN,DHIN DHĀ /
0
DHĀ GHE,TIRA KIṬA TIN TIN,TIN TĀ /
3
TĀ KE,TIRA KIṬA DHIN DHIN,DHIN DHĀ,TE//

Memorise these two kisme and then try to create your own way of decorating the theka.

4. *The Tihai*

Tihāī is a cadential formula that consists of a pattern of strokes, the tihai phrase, repeated successively exactly three times. It may begin on any matra and normally ends on sam. The final stroke of the tihai is the point at which the tension built up by the tihai is resolved, and that stroke is usually DHĀ.

There are two rests between the repetitions of the tihai phrase. These rests must be equal in duration. If the rests are more in duration than one matra each, the tihai is known as *dumdār.* If the rests are each one matra or less in duration then the tihai is known as *bedumdār.*

Tihai is an improvised form and requires great skill and command of tal to perform. Until you are an accomplished artist you will be limited to using tihais you have rehearsed and know very well.

In the following tihai, the tihai phrase is TAKA TIRA KIṬA TAKA DHĀ. It is 5 matras long and when repeated three times with two rests of 1 matra each, a tihai 17 matras long is made i.e. one cycle of tintal plus sam. The tihai phrase is bracketed.

TIHAI 1

+ 2
(TAKA TIRA KIṬA TAKA / DHĀ) S TAKA TIRA /
0 3
KIṬA TAKA DHĀ S / TAKA TIRA KITA TAKA//
+
DHĀ

Here is another dumdar tihai that takes two cycles of tintal to be completed. The tihai phrase DHĀ TIRA KIṬA TAKA TAKA DHĀ TIRA KIṬA DHĀ is 9 matras long. In order that on the third repetition the final DHA coincides with sam, the two rests have each to be 3 matras long. The tihai phrase is bracketed.

TIHAI 2

```
+                                    2
(DHĀ TIRA KIṬA TAKA / TAKA DHĀ TIRA KIṬA /
                                     3
DHĀ) S    S    S     / DHĀ TIRA KIṬA TAKA /
                                     2
TAKA DHĀ TIRA KIṬA / DHĀ S    S    S     /
                                     3
DHĀ TIRA KIṬA TAKA / TAKA DHĀ TIRA KIṬA //
+
DHĀ
```

From tihai 1 and tihai 2 you have learnt two formulae for making tihais. They both begin on sam and both are dumdar.

```
TIHAI 1      (- - - - / DHĀ S) x 3
              +         2

TIHAI 2      (- - - - / - - - - / DHĀ S S S /) x 3
              +         2         0
```

Tihai 3 is one cycle long. The rests are each less than 1 matra in duration so it is bedumdar. The tihai phrase which is 5½ matras long has been bracketed.

TIHAI 3

```
+
(DHĀ,TIRA   KIṬA,TAKA   TIN,NĀ      KIṬA,TAKA /
2
DHĀ,TE      DHĀ,)DHĀ    TIRA,KIṬA   TAKA,TIN /
0
NĀ,KIṬA     TAKA,DHĀ    TE,DHĀ      DHĀ,TIRA /
3
KIṬA,TAKA   TIN,NĀ      KIṬA,TAKA   DHĀ,TE //
+
DHĀ
```

Tihai 4 is two cycles long. The tihai phrase which is bracketed includes a tihai. The rest between the repetitions is 1 matra so the tihai is bedumdar.

TIHAI 4

```
+
(DHĀ,TIRA   KIṬA,TAKA   TIN,NĀ      KIṬA,TAKA /
2
DHĀ         TIN,NĀ      KIṬA,TAKA   DHĀ /
0
TIN,NĀ      KIṬA,TAKA   DHĀ )       DHĀ,TIRA /
3
KIṬA,TAKA   TIN,NĀ      KIṬA,TAKA   DHĀ //
+
TIN,NĀ      KIṬA,TAKA   DHĀ         TIN,NĀ /
2
KIṬA,TAKA   DHĀ         DHĀ,TIRA    KIṬA,TAKA /
0
TIN,NĀ      KIṬA,TAKA   DHĀ         TIN,NĀ /
3
KIṬA,TAKA   DHĀ         TIN,NĀ      KIṬA,TAKA //
+
DHĀ
```

Here are the formulae for these two bedumbar tihais.

TIHAI 3 (- - - - / - DHĀ,) x 3

TIHAI 4 (- - - - / - - - - / - - DHĀ) x 3
+ 2 0

An important function of tihai is to conclude the improvisations of a kayada. Such a tihai is normally derived from its final palta. Here is a palta of kayada 1 followed by a tihai using the formula for tihai 1..

Palta

+ TE,TE	GHI,TE	TE,GHI	GHI,GHI	/
2 GHI,GHI	TE,TE	GHI,GHI	TIRA,KITA	/
0 TE,TE	KI,TE	TE,KI	KI,KI	/
3 GHI,GHI	TE,TE	GHI,GHI	TIRA,KITA	//

Tihai

+ (TE,TE	GHI,TE	TE,GHI	GHI,GHI	/
2 DHA)	S	TE,TE	GHI,TE	/
0 TE,GHI	GHI,GHI	DHA	S	/
3 TE,TE	GHI,TE	TE,GHI	GHI,GHI	//
+ DHA				

The following example uses the tihai formula 2. It is based on palta 6 of kayada 2:-

+ (DHA,DHA	DHA,DHA	TE,TE	TE,TE	/
2 DHA,DHA	TE,TE	DHA,DHA	TIN,NA	/
0 DHA)	S	S	S	/
3 DHA,DHA	DHA,DHA	TE,TE	TE,TE	//
+ DHA,DHA	TE,TE	DHA,DHA	TIN,NA	/
2 DHA	S	S	S	/
0 DHA,DHA	DHA,DHA	TE,TE	TE,TE	/
3 DHA,DHA	TE,TE	DHA, DHA	TIN,NA	//
+ DHA				

Tihais, like paltas, should be in the same layakari as the kayada theme. Here is a bedumdar tihai to follow palta 5 of kayada 5. It is in ari layakari. This tihai uses tihai formula 4.

Tihai

+				
(DHA,TIRA,KITA	DHA,GHE,NA	DHA,GHE,TI	NA,KI,NA	/
2				
DHA	DHA,GHE,TI	NA,KI,NA	DHA	/
0				
DHA,GHE,TI	NA,KI,NA	DHA)	DHA,TIRA,KITA	/
3				
DHA,GHE,NA	DHA,GHE,TI	NA,KI,NA	DHA	//
+				
DHA,GHE,TI	NA,KI,NA	DHA	DHA,GHE,TI	/
2				
NA,KI,NA	DHA	DHA,TIRA,KITA	DHA,GHE,NA	/
0				
DHA,GHE,TI	NA,KI,NA	DHA	DHA,GHE,TI	/
3				
NA,KI,NA	DHA	DHA,GHE,TI	NA,KI,NA	//
+				
DHA				

Now create your own tihais, deriving them from the kayadas and paltas you know.

5. Riaz Schedules

Here are two schedules — one of thirty minutes and one of sixty minutes. Every kayada is first to be played several times thah then dun. Then practise chaugun for as long as possible. Chaugun is to be the fastest speed at which you can play the kayada correctly. For a longer practice schedule increase the time spent playing the kayada chaugun and playing the paltas.

Remember to play this schedule without any breaks. Check your fingering, making sure your speed is constant and that every stroke is evenly spaced.

Practise playing the DHĀs in kayadas 2 and 3 as you learnt in 'NĀ DIN DIN NĀ' i.e. with the ring finger still in contact with the syahi. This will enable you to increase the tempo at which you can play kayadas 2 and 3.

30 MINUTES DAILY

5 mins.	Kayada 2.
6 mins.	Practise each palta several times. End with tihai played once.
5 mins.	Kayada 3.
6 mins.	Play each palta several times. End with tihai played once.
5 mins.	Kayada 4.
2 mins.	Practise palta 1 for one minute and palta 2 for one minute. End with a tihai based on palta 2.

60 MINUTES DAILY.

5 mins.	Kayada 2.
10 mins.	Practise paltas 1 to 5 plus some of your own. Repeat each one several times. End with an appropriate tihai, basing it on the last palta you play and using a tihai formula you know.
5 mins.	Kayada 3.
5 mins.	Practise paltas for kayada 3. End with an appropriate tihai played once.
5 mins.	Kayada 4
10 mins.	Practise paltas for kayada 4. End with an appropriate tihai played once.
2 mins.	Kayada 5 in derhgun
3 mins.	Kayada 5 in tigun
5 mins.	Practise paltas for kayada 5 at the same tempo. End with tihai played once.
5 mins.	Kisme of tintal in vilambit laya
5 mins.	Tintal theka in madhya laya

A major portion of the career of professional tabla players is spent accompanying various vocal, instrumental and dance styles. But their training is in the art of solo playing. Only when they are accomplished artists do they learn the accompaniment styles, such as for Khyal, Ghazal, Kathak dance etc. by rehearsing and performing with other musicians.

The tabla solo consists of several movements, each having one or more type of piece — some improvised and some composed. It can be performed in any tal. But a solo performance consists of the pieces and movements played in one tal only, the laya of which is increased as the performance progresses. The pieces and movements are separated by theka.

The Banaras *gharānā* (school of tabla playing) is famous for its tabla solos, which can be five hours or more in length. The soloist is accompanied on a melody instrument which plays a time-keeping pattern called *laharā*. Here is a very popular lahara written out in Indian *sargam* notation and western staff notation systems.

Lahara

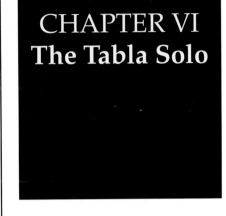

CHAPTER VI
The Tabla Solo

1. Bhumika and uthan

In the Banaras gharana, a solo performance is begun with the improvised form, *bhumikā*. The bhumika is a slow piece in which the use of bold stroking on the dahina is contrasted with the use of the soft band stroke KI of the baya.

Here is a typical example of the opening phrases a tabla player would use in a bhumika. It is to be played one bol to a matra in the laya chosen and at least twice.

NOTE that in playing the stroke KRA the right hand follows the left hand in quick succession. And TIRA,KIṬA is played twice as fast as TĀ,KE

Bhumika — Layakari - barabar

	+			
	TE	TĀṄ	S	KĪ
D:	2	4		
B:				-
	2			
	KĪ	TE	TĀ,KE	TIRA,KIṬA
D:	-	2	4	2 3 2
B:			-	-
	0			
	TE	TĀṄ	KĪ,KĪ	TE,ṬE
D:	3	4		2 3
B:			- -	
	3			
	TE,ṬE	TĀ S,S KRA	TET,TĀ	TIRA,KIṬA
D:	2 3	4 2	3 4	2 3 2
B:		-		-

In performance the bhumika is immediately followed by an *uthan*. The uthan is a virtuoso piece with which tabla players demonstrate their technical skills on their instrument. The introduction of the khula baya stroke GHE of an uthan dramatically changes the mood from that created in the bhumika section.

The uthan would normally be improvised by an experienced artist. But it is one of the more difficult tabla forms to execute and there are many composed uthans of varying degrees of difficulty.

The following uthan is one taught to beginners. It uses only the strokes taught in the first three kayadas, though some of the bols are different. DIN is stroke 5, TI is stroke 2, and DHE is stroke 3 plus GHE. This composition is to be played as much as eight times as fast as the bhumika but not less than twice as fast.

Uthan — Layakari - barabar

	+				
	DHĀ,TE	TE,DHĀ	TE,TE	DHĀ,GHE	|
D:	6 2	3 6	2 3	6	
B:	^	^		^ ^	

	2				
	TE,TE	KATA,DHĀ	TE,TE	DHĀ,GHE	|
D:	2 3	2 6	2 3	6	
B:		- ^		^ ^	

	0				
	DIN,S	DIN,S	NĀ,NĀ	TE,TE	|
D:	5	5	6 6	2 3	
B:					

	3				
	GHE,NĀ	TE,TE	GHE,NĀ	TIN,NĀ	||
D:	6	2 3	6	5 6	
B:	^		^		

	+				
	KA,TIRA	KITA,DHE	TE,TE	DHĀ,GHE	|
D:	2 3	2 3	2 3	6	
B:	-	- ^		^ ^	

	2				
	TE,TE	KA,TE	TE,DHĀ	S,TI	|
D:	2 3	2	3 6	2	
B:		-	^		

0	DHĀ,S	KA,TE	TE,DHĀ	S,TI	/
3	DHĀ,S	KA,TE	TE,DHĀ	S,TI	//
+	DHĀ,S	S,DHE	TE,TE	DHĀ,GHE	/
2	TE,TE	KA,TE	TE,DHĀ	S,TI	/
0	DHĀ,S	KA,TE	TE,DHĀ	S,TI	/
3	DHĀ,S	KA,TE	TE,DHĀ	S,TI	//
+	DHĀ,S	S,DHE	TE,TE	DHĀ,GHE	/
2	TE,TE	KA,TE	TE,DHĀ	S,TI	/
0	DHĀ,S	KA,TE	TE,DHĀ	S,TI	/
3	DHĀ,S	KA,TE	TE,DHĀ	S,TI	//
+	DHĀ				

2. Mohara and Mukhra

The second movement of the tabla solo consists of short pieces (less than a cycle in length) that show the sam. These pieces can be either *moharās* or *mukhṛās*. They are improvised and started on any matra of the tal. As with uthan, there are several composed pieces in this form.

The mohara begins with a short introduction that is followed with a tihai. The beginning of the tihai is marked with an asterisk.

Mohara   Layakari - barabar

Tali: 0
Matra: 9 ‾   10 ‾
        DHĀ S,TIN   NĀ   KITA TAKA,TĀ TIRA
    D: 6   5   6   2 ˙3   6 2 3
    B: ^   -   -

Matra: 11   *   12
        KITA TAKA,TIRA KIṬA   TAKA TAKA,TIRA KIṬA
    D: 2˙   3   2 3   2˙   3   3   2 3   ˙2
    B: -   -   -   -   -   -

Tali: 3
Matra: 13 ‾   14
        DHĀ S,TIRA KIṬA   TAKA TAKA,TIRA KIṬA
    D: 6   2 3   2˙   3   3   2 3   2˙
    B: ^   -   -   -   -

Matra: 15 ‾   16
        DHĀ S,TIRA KIṬA   TAKA TAKA,TIRA KIṬA
    D: 6   2 3   2˙   3   3   2 3   2˙
    B: ^   -   -   -   -

Tali: +
Matra: 1 ‾
        DHĀ
    D: 6
    B: ^

The *mukhṛā* is similar to the mohara but without the tihai. The following mukhra is in ari layakari. In it there is a new bol phrase, GHIN S, TA RĀ, S NA. GHIN is the same stroke as GHE. TA, RĀ and NA are explained on pages 44 to 47.

This stroke is like TE (2) but played on the chanti.

- ☐ **Learning position of stroke:** See Fig. 21a.
  Place the tips of the middle and ring fingers on the chanti. Hold the index finger a little distance away from the middle and ring fingers and above the puri. Keep the wrist firm.
- ☐ **Executing the stroke:** See Fig. 21a.
  Raise the forearm vertically into the air. Let it drop while rotating the outside of the forearm slightly downwards and strike the chanti with the middle and ring fingers. Keep the wrist firm and level with the hand and forearm.
- ☐ **Final position of hand:** See Fig. 21b.
  Let the hand remain in position on the chanti.

Right: Figure 21a

Opposite: Figure 21b

DAHINA
Khulla Bol: TA or NA
Stroke No.: 7

This stroke is like ṬE (3) but played on the chanti.

- ☐ **Learning position of stroke:** See Fig 22a.

  Place the tip of the index finger on the chanti. Hold the middle and ring fingers a little distance away from the index finger and above the puri. Keep the wrist firm.

- ☐ **Executing the stroke:** See Fig 22a.

  Raise the arm vertically into the air. Let it drop while rotating the inside edge of the forearm slightly downwards and strike the chanti with the index finger. Keep the wrist firm and level with the hand and forearm.

- ☐ **Final position of stroke:**

  Let the hand remain in position on the chanti.

N.B. In playing the strokes TA RĀ S NA, there is a gap between the index and middle fingers.

Right: Fig. 22a

Opposite: Fig. 22b

DAHINA
Dahina Bol: RA or R̄A
Stroke No.: 8

MUKHRA

Layakari: ari

tali:	0	
matra:	9	10
	TA,KA,TIN	NĀ,KIṬA,TAKA
D:	2 5	6 2 3
B:	-	- -
matra	11	12
	TIRA,KIṬA,TAKA	TAKA,TIRA,KIṬA
D:	2 3 2 3	3 2 3 2
B:	- -	- -
tali: 3		
matra:	13	14
	GHIN S,TARĀ,S NA	DHĀ S,TIRA,KIṬA
D:	7 8 7	6 2 3 2
B:	^	^ -
matra:	15	16
	DHĀ TIRA,KIṬA DHE,TE ṬE	KATA,GIDA,GINA
D:	6 2 3 2 3 2 3	5 2 3
B:	^ - ^	- ^ ^
tali:	+	
matra:	1	
	DHĀ	
D:	6	
B:	^	

3. Bant

Kayada is an important part of a solo performance. In the Banaras gharana performance kayadas are also referred to as *bāṅṭ*. Here is a bant that is often heard in performances. It uses the two NĀ's as in tintal theka.

This bant has been written out in dugun and the paltas in dugun. In performing, make sure that the laya of the tal is at a tempo that allows you to play the paltas in this layakari.

BANT

	+			
	DHI,GA	DHI,NĀ	TIRA,KIṬA	DHI,NĀ
D:	4	4 6	2 3 2	4 6
B:	^ ^	^	-	^
	2			
	DHĀ,GE	NĀ,TI	KA,TI	NĀ,NĀ
D:	6	6 4	4	6 6
B:	^ ^	-	- -	
	0			
	TI,KA	TI,NĀ	TIRA,KIṬA	DHI,NĀ
D:	4	4 6	2 3 2	4 6
B:	- -	-	-	^
	3			
	DHĀ,GHE	NĀ,DHI	GA,DHI	NĀ,NĀ
D:	6	6 4	4	6 6
B:	^ ^	^	^ ^	

Palta

1.

DHI,GA	DHI,NA	TIRA,KITA	DHI,NA
DHI,GA	DHI,NA	TIRA,KITA	DHI,NA
*DHI,GA	DHI,NA	TIRA,KITA	DHI,NA
DHA,GE	NA,TI	KA,TI	NA,NA
mundi			

2.

DHI,GA	DHI,NA	TIRA,KITA	DHI,NA
TIRA,KITA	DHI,NA	TIRA,KITA	DHI,NA
*DHI,GA	DHI,NA	TIRA,KITA	DHI,NA
DHA,GE	NA,TI	KA,TI	NA,NA
mundi			

3.

DHI,GA	DHI,NA	TIRA,KITA	DHI,NA
TIRA,KITA	TIRA,KITA	TIRA,KITA	DHI,NA
*DHI,GA	DHI,NA	TIRA,KITA	DHI,NA
DHA,GE	NA,TI	KA,TI	NA,NA
mundi			

4.

DHI,GA	DHI,NA	TIRA,KITA	DHI,NA
TIRA,KITA	TIRA,KITA	DHIN,NA	TIRA,KITA
*DHI,GA	DHI,NA	TIRA,KITA	DHI,NA
DHA,GE	NA,TI	KA,TI	NA,NA
mundi			

5.

DHI,GA	DHI,NA	TIRA,KITA	DHI,NA
TIRA,KITA	TAKA,TIRA	KITA,TAKA	DHI,NA
*DHI,GA	DHI,NA	TIRA,KITA	DHI,NA
DHA,GE	NA,TI	KA,TI	NA,NA
mundi			

6.

TIRA,KITA	TAKA,TIRA	KITA,TAKA	DHI,NA
DHA,GE	NA,TI	KA,TI	NA,NA
*DHI,GA	DHI,NA	TIRA,KITA	DHI,NA
DHA,GE	NA,TI	KA,TI	NA,NA
mundi			

7.

TIRA,KITA	TAKA,TIRA	KITA,TAKA	DHI,NA
TIRA,KITA	DHI,NA	TIRA,KITA	DHI,NA
*DHI,GA	DHI,NA	TIRA,KITA	DHI,NA
DHA,GE	NA,TI	KA,TI	NA,NA
mundi			

8.

TIRA,KITA	DHI,NA	TIRA,KITA	DHI,NA
TIRA,KITA	DHI,NA	TIRA,KITA	DHI,NA
*DHI,GA	DHI,NA	TIRA,KITA	DHI,NA
DHA,GE	NA,TI	KA,TI	NA,NA
mundi			

9.

TIRA,KITA	TIRA,KITA	DHI,NA	TIRA,KITA
TIRA,KITA	DHI,NA	TIRA,KITA	DHI,NA
*DHI,GA	DHI,NA	TIRA,KITA	DHI,NA
DHA,GE	NA,TI	KA,TI	NA,NA
mundi			

TIHAI

This is a dumdar tihai with a tihai phrase of 21 matras and a rest of one matra between the repetitions of the tihai phrase.

tali bol

+	TIRA,KITA	TIRA,KITA	DHI,NA	TIRA,KITA	/
2	TIRA,KITA	DHI,NA	TIRA,KITA	TIRA,KITA	/
0	DHI,NA	TIRA,KITA	TIRA,KITA	DHI,NA	/
3	DHI,GA	DHI,NA	TIRA,KITA	DHI,NA	//
+	DHA,GE	NA,TI	KA,TI	NA,NA	/
2	DHA	S	TIRA,KITA	TIRA,KITA	/
0	DHI,NA	TIRA,KITA	TIRA,KITA	DHI,NA	/
3	TIRA,KITA	TIRA,KITA	DHI,NA	TIRA,KITA	//
+	TIRA,KITA	DHI,NA	DHI,GA	DHI,NA	/
2	TIRA,KITA	DHI,NA	DHA,GE	NA,TI	/
0	KA,TI	NA,NA	DHA	S	/
3	TIRA,KITA	TIRA,KITA	DHI,NA	TIRA,KITA	//
+	TIRA,KITA	DHI,NA	TIRA,KITA	TIRA,KITA	/
2	DHI,NA	TIRA,KITA	TIRA,KITA	DHI,NA	/
0	DHI,GA	DHI,NA	TIRA,KITA	DHI,NA	/
3	DHA,GE	NA,TI	KA,TI	NA,NA	//
+	DHA				

4.   Rela

Kayada is normally followed in performance by a *relā*. The rela has the same structure and form as kayada but has its bols arranged in such a way that it can be played at least four times as fast as a kayada.

The following rela introduces a very important bol of tabla playing — DHERE. An artist's ability to play this bol quickly and clearly is an important asset and long hours of practice are required to perfect it. A description of how to play it is on pages 51 and 52.

NOTE   that   <u>DHERE, DHERE</u>   is   actually   played <u>DHERE,TERE</u> to enable it to be played quickly.

Rela   Layakari - Barabar.

```
        +
        DHĀ,TIRA      KIṬA,TAKA      DHERE,DHERE     KIṬA,TAKA
D:      6     2 3        2   3       9   10 9   10     2   3
B:      ^                -       -   ^                 -       -

        2
        DHĀ,TIRA      KIṬA,TAKA      TIN,NĀ          KIṬA,TAKA
D:      6     2 3        2   3       5    6            2   3
B:      ^                -       -                     -       -

        0
        TĀ,TIRA       KIṬA,TAKA      TERE,TERE       KIṬA,TAKA
D:      6   2 3          2   3       9 10 9 10         2   3
B:                      -       -                     -       -

        3
        DHĀ,TIRA      KIṬA,TAKA      DHIN,NĀ         KIṬA,TAKA
D:      6     2 3        2   3       5    6            2   3
B:      ^                -       -   ^                 -       -
```

NOTE: TERE is usually played in sequence, in which case RE (10) becomes the initial position for TE (9).

To play this stroke effectively allow the elbow to move freely inwards and then outwards.

- ☐ **Learning position of stroke:** See Fig 23a

  Place the fleshy part of the thumb and base of index finger on the inner edge of the syahi. Keep the rest of the palm and other fingers off the puri.

- ☐ **Executing the stroke:** See Fig. 23b.

  Hit the outer edge of the syahi with the fleshy part of the outer edge of the palm while rotating the outer edge of the forearm downwards. Ensure that the rest of the palm and the other fingers do not come in contact with the puri.

- ☐ **Final position of hand:**

  Let the hand remain firmly, without tension, in this position on the drumhead.

Previous page: Figure. 23a

Right: Figure 23b

DAHINA
Band Bol: TE
Stroke No. 9

- **Learning position of stroke:** See Fig 23b.

  Place the edge of the palm and little finger on the outer edge of the syahi. Keep the rest of the palm and other fingers off the puri.

- **Executing the stroke:** See Fig. 24.

  Hit the inner edge of the syahi with the fleshy part of the thumb and the base of the index fingers while rotating the inner edge of the forearm downwards. Ensure that the rest of the palm and the other fingers do not come in contact with the puri.

- **Final position of hand:**

  Let the hand remain in this position firmly on the drumhead.

5. Riaz schedules

Create your own schedule according to the minimum time you have available each day. Kayadas 2, 3, and 4 are to be played thah, dun, and chaugun. Kayada 5 is to be played derhgun, tigun and chhagun.

Add tintal to the end of your practice schedule. Practise the theka as long as possible every day in the same way as you practice kayada i.e. thah, dun and chaugun.

End you riaz with as many compositions as you have time to practise. Play each one repeatedly for at least five minutes.

Right: Figure 24

DAHINA
Band Bol: RE
Stroke No. 10

The final movement of a tabla solo is made up of many different types of compositions, usually very old and composed by famous musicians of the past. Some were composed for the tabla and others for the *pakhāwaj.*

The pakhawaj is a barrel-shaped drum traditionally used to accompany certain classical styles of music and dance, such as dhrupad, and orissi dance (see fig. 2). The pakhawaj has a loud and sombre tone, in contrast to the softer sound of the tabla. When performing the pakhawaj compositions on the tabla, a player uses some of the strokes of that instrument and a large number of khula strokes.

1. Gat

Gats are the oldest compositions in a tabla player's repertoire and were composed by musicians in the past, many of whom are known. They have the same khuli-mundi form of kayada and in performance are played more than once in different layakari. The bol phrases of a gat are generally more difficult than those of kayada and are a test of an artist's technical skills. These pieces are beautiful examples of rhythmic composition and allow tabla players to demonstrate their interpretative skills and musicality. In a performance they are usually played at different laya and layakari.

The following gat has no new strokes but many new bols. This is typical of gats as they were composed by musicians coming from many different traditions of tabla playing. This gat is in ari layakari. It has been notated in tigun.

CHAPTER VII
Tabla and Pakhawaj Bols

GAT Layakari - ari

```
       +
       KA,S,TA            DHE,TE,ṬE   KA,TA,GĪ   DA,GĪ,NA     |
  D:       2              3    2 3̇       2       5      2     |
  B:   -                  ^              -    ^       ^       |

       2
       DHĀ,TIRA,KIṬA      DHE,TE,ṬE   KA,TA,GĪ   DA,GĪ,NA     |
  D:   6     2 3     2̇    3    2 3̇       2       5      6     |
  B:   ^           -      ^              -    ^       ^       |

       0
       NA,RA,NA           RA,NA,RA    TE,ṬE,TE   ṬE,TE,ṬE     |
  D:   8  7  8            7  8  7     3  2̇  3    2̇  3  2̇      |
  B:                                                          |

       3
       *DHĀ,TIRA,KIṬA     DHE,TE,ṬE   KA,TA,GĪ   DA,GĪ,NA     ||
  D:   6     2 3     2̇    3    2 3̇       3       5      6     ||
  B:   ^           -      ^              -    ^       ^       ||
       mundi
```

2. Tukara

Next to the kayada, the *ṭukaṛā* is the most commonly heard tabla piece. It has the same form as the mohara but is never less in length than one cycle of a tal. Great masters of tabla playing usually use composed tukaras as a theme and compose their own variations on them, often on the spur of the moment in a performance.

A tukara is played only once in a solo and at the fastest possible speed. It may have bol phrases in different layakari. In the following example TA,KI,TA is in ari layakari and the other phrases are in barabar layakari.

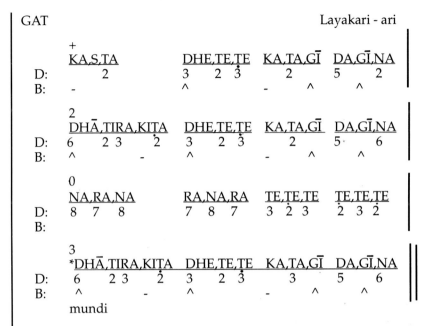

Tukara

+				
DHERE,DHERE	KIṬA,TAKA	TA,KI,TA	DHĀ	/

D: 9   10   2   3   3   2   6

B: ^   -   -   -   ^

2				
DHERE,DHERE	KIṬA,TAKA	TA,KI,TA	DHĀ	/

0				
TA,KI,TA	DHĀ	TA,KI,TA	DHĀ	/

3				
DHERE,DHERE	KIṬA,TAKA	TA,KI,TA	DHĀ	//

+				
KA	DHERE,DHERE	KIṬA,TAKA	TA,KI,TA	/

2				
DHĀ	S	KA	DHERE,DHERE	/

0				
KIṬA,TAKA	TA,KI,TA	DHĀ	S	/

3				
KA	DHERE,DHERE	KIṬA,TAKA	TA,KI,TA	//

+
DHĀ

3. Chakkradar tukara

Chakkradār tukaras consist of a piece in the form of a tukara that is repeated three times in such a way that the final DHĀ coincides with sam. It is played only once in a performance, at the fastest possible speed. In the following example the tukara is bracketed.

Chakkradar Tukara

+				
(DHERE,DHERE	KIṬA,TAKA	TA,KI,TA	DHĀ	/

2				
DHERE,DHERE	KIṬA,TAKA	TA,KI,TA	DHĀ	/

0				
TA,KI,TA	DHĀ	TA,KI,TA	DHĀ	/

3				
DHERE,DHERE	KIṬA,TAKA	TA,KI,TA	DHĀ	//

+				
KA	DHERE,DHERE	KIṬA,TAKA	TA,KI,TA	/

2				
DHĀ	TI	DHĀ	KA	/

0				
DHERE,DHERE	KIṬA,TAKA	TA,KI,TA	DHĀ	/

3				
TI	DHĀ	KA	DHERE,DHERE	//

+				
KIṬA,TAKA	TA,KI,TA	DHĀ	TI	/

2			
DHĀ	S)	X	3

4. Paran

Paran is a pakhawaj form. It has many khula strokes. The paran has the same structure and is performed in the same way as the tukara — once only as quickly as possible. The following paran can be the basis of numerous variations.

Paran

```
      +
      DHA,DHA    DIN,DIN    NA,NA     TETE,TETE /
D:    4    4     5   5      6   6     2 3  2 3
B:    ^    ^

      2
      KATE,TEKA  TETE,KATA  DHA,KATA  DHA,KATA /
D:      2  3     2  3   2   6     2   6     2
B:    -    -        -       ^   -     ^   -

      0
      DHA S,S KA TETE,KATA  DHA,KATA  DHA,KATA /

      3
      DHA S,S KA TETE,KATA  DHA,KATA  DHA,KATA //

      +
      DHA
```

5. Chakkradar paran

Here is a chakkradar paran derived from the above paran.

Chakkradar Paran

```
+
(DHA,DHA    DHA,DIN    DIN,DIN    NA,NA

2
NA,TETE     TETE,TETE  KATE,TEKA  TETE,KATA

0
DHA,KATA    DHA,KATA   DHA ) x 3
```

6. The length of time it will have taken you to complete this manual will depend on the degree of proficiency you wished to achieve in the execution of the basic strokes and elementary pieces. You will require several more years of training before you can become an accomplished tabla player.

Notes on the pronunciation of Indian words:

The scheme of transliteration is as follows:-

Pronounce 'a' as in 'India',	'e' as 'a' as in 'say'
'ā' as in 'far'	'o' as in 'pole'
'i' as in 'bit',	'u' as in 'full',
'ī' as 'ee' in 'meet'	'ū' as 'oo' in 'room'

Consonants are pronounced approximately as in English.

The main exceptions are:

1. Consonants with a dot under them are pronounced with the tongue touching the palate.
2. Consonants followed by 'h' are aspirated.
   e.g. bh, ph, th, ṭh, dh, ḍh, rh are all strongly aspirated
   Note: chh as in 'chair' but strongly aspirated
3. ṛ is retroflex
4. ṅ is nasal

GLOSSARY

Ardh Virām:- A comma used in Bhatkhande notation to divide the matra into sections of equal duration.

Āṛī:- The playing of a piece ¾, 1½, 3, 6. etc. times as fast as the speed of a tal.

Āvartan:- One complete cycle of a tal.

Baddhī:- Leather strap on a tabla.

Banaras:- One of the seven holy cities of the Hindus. It is situated on the banks of the Ganges. It is now called Varanasi (its original name) which is taken from two neighbouring rivulets, the Varana and the Asi.

Baṅd (of tabla strokes):- Dampened, muted.

Bāṅṭ:- Same as kayada; the performance kayada of the Banaras gharana.

Barābar:- The playing of a piece at 1, 2, 4, etc. times as the speed of the tal.

Bāyā:- The small kettle drum of the tabla pair.

Bedamdār (of a tihai):- Without pauses.

Bhumikā (in tabla tradition):- A rhythmic form that uses the closed bols of the tabla and opens a solo performance.

Bol:- Mnemonic syllable used for oral notation of tabla strokes: a rhythmic phrase (on the tabla); a tabla composition: a tune.

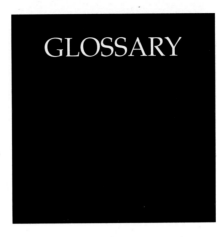

Chakkaradār:- A piece (usually tukara or paran) consisting of three identical parts, each ending with a tihai.

Chāṅtī:- The rim of the tabla head.

Chaugun:- The playing of a piece four times as fast as the speed of the tal.

Dahinā:- The (upside down) conical-shaped drum of the tabla pair.

Damdār:- (of a tihai) with pauses.

Drut:- (in sangit tradition) quick tempo.

Dugun:- The playing of a piece twice as fast as the tal.

Dūn:- Fast tempo; the fastest speed at which you can play a piece.

Gajarā:- The lacing that holds the skins of a tabla head together.

Gat:- (in tabla tradition) a rhythmic form usually consisting of two halves, the second half a modification of the first; a piece composed by musicians of previous generations.

Gattā:- See gittak.

Giṭṭak:- Wooden dowels used to tune the dahina.

Giralī:- Ring used to hold the tabla at the desired angle for playing.

Gun:- Equivalent to 'times' in the system of layakari.

Hathauṛī:- A special hammer used to tune the tabla.

Kāyadā:- (in tabla tradition) a rhythmic form consisting of two halves, the second half a modification of the first; a composition in this form; a composition and its variations in this form; a teaching composition in this form.

Khālī:- The least stressed beat of a tal.

Khulā:- (of tabla strokes) ringing, resonant.

Khulī:- (in tabla tradition) the first half of certain rhythmic forms.

Laharā:- A time-keeping melody.

Lao:- The complete skin of a puri; the exposed skin of the puri between the syahi and the chanti.

Lakaṛī:- The body of a tabla.

Layakārī:- System of dividing the matra.

Madhya: (in sangit tradition) medium tempo.

Maidān:- Same as lao.

Mātrā:- One beat of a tal cycle.

Moharā:- (in tabla tradition) a rhythmic form, consisting of a rhythmic passage and tihai being a ½ cycle or less in length; a composed piece or improvised piece in this form.

Mukhṛā:- (in tabla tradition) a rhythmic form; a composed piece used to point out sam.

Muṅḍī:- (in tabla tradition) the second half of certain rhythmic forms;

Palṭā:- (in tabla tradition) the variations on a theme.

Paran:- (in tabla tradition) a rhythmic form being one cycle or more in length; a composed or improvised piece in this form; a piece comprised of pakhawaj bols.

Peṅch:- A type of palta.

Relā:- (in tabla tradition) a rhythmic form consisting of two halves, the second a modification of the first; a composition in this form; a composition and variations on it each in this form; a composition and variations that sound like a train running on tracks.

Saṅgīt:- The technical term for music and dance.

Sam:- The strongest beat of a tal, the first beat of a tal.

Syāhī:- The black spot on the tabla head.

Tablā:- A pair of tuned drums used for solo playing and as the main instrument of accompaniment in the music and dance of North India.

Tāl:- A time cycle; a technical term for the rhythmic system of Indian music; a clapping of hands.

Tālī:- The stressed beats, the claps (and waves) of a tal.

Ṭhāh:- Slow tempo; half the fastest speed at which a piece is to be played.

Ṭhekā:- The time-keeping pattern of a tal played on the tabla.

Tigun:- The playing of a piece three times as fast as the speed of a tal.

Tihāī:- An improvised or composed phrase that is repeated three times with or without pauses in between so that the final beat of the phrase on its third repetition coincides with a predetermined beat of the tal in which it is being played.

Ṭukaṛa:- (in tabla tradition) a rhythmic form consisting of a rhythmic passage and tihai; a composed or improvised piece in this form; a piece comprising of tabla bols.

Uṭhān:- (in tabla tradition) a rhythmic form consisting of a rhythmic passage and tihai; a composed or improvised piece in this form; an improvised piece that follows the bhumika of a solo performance that may have more than one tihai.

Vibhāg:- A subdivision of a tal consisting of a fixed number of matras.

Vilambit:- (in sangit tradition) slow tempo.

THE AUTHORS

Pandit Sharda Sahai is the direct descendant of Pandit Ram Sahai who founded the Banaras Gharana of tabla playing in the latter part of the 18th century. He was born in Banaras, India, in the ancestral home and learned tabla from his father, Bhagvati Sahai until he died when Sharda Sahai was about eight years old. He then became a student of Kanthe Maharaj, whose Guru was Baldeo Sahai, Sharda Sahai's grandfather.

Sharda-ji began his professional career at the age of nine, performing as both soloist and accompanist. He made his major public debut at sixteen, appearing at the Italee Music Conference in Calcutta with the sarod maestro, Ali Akbar Khan. Since then he has played thousands of concerts world-wide. As an accompanist he has performed with every major artist in India. He has also made his name as a soloist and has played for the prestigious National programme of All India Radio.

Sharda-ji has frequently toured the West as a soloist and as accompanist to visiting artists from India. He also takes part in a wide variety of cross-cultural and experimental musical programmes. He has performed with South Indian musicians, with such *avant garde* composers as John Cage, and with the internationally acclaimed percussion group Nexus. He is presently a member of the 'World Drums' ensemble which brings together many of the leading percussion specialists of music cultures from around the world.

From 1970 to 1976 he was Artist in Residence with the World Music programme at Wesleyan University in Connecticut, USA and visiting artist at Brown University in Rhode Island and at the Berklee School of Music in Boston. In 1975-1976 he received a grant from the John D. Rockefeller III Fund to be the Resident Artist at Brown University in Rhode Island. In September 1985 Sharda-ji accepted an invitation to be Senior Lecturer at the Dartington College of Arts in Totnes, Devon.

In 1965 Sharda-ji set up the Pt. Ram Sahai Sangit Vidyalaya in Banaras to enable students to learn from professional musicians and dancers without the constraints of the guru-disciple relationship. While in the UK he helped Frances Shepherd to found a charitable trust, named after his school in Banaras, to contribute to the development of Indian music in the UK.

His solo performances can be heard on *The Art of the Benares Baj* (World Records, 1983) and *The Music of Asia* (WOMAD, 1987).

Dr Frances Shepherd is a disciple of Sharda Sahai. She became his pupil in America in 1972, where she was studying for a Ph.D. in ethnomusicology. She then became his teaching assistant and worked with him in developing a method of instructing students in the West in tabla playing, both in America and India.

Frances is from Guyana, South America. She first came to the UK in 1963 to complete her schooling, then went to Dartington College of Arts in Devon where she studied western music. While there she had her first lessons in Indian music theory from Professor Nazir Jairazbhoy, in sitar playing from Ustad Imrat Khan, and in tabla from Lateef Ahmed Khan. She was familiar with the popular and devotional forms of Indian music which were an important aspect of musical life in her native Guyana.

In 1971 she accepted an invitation from Professor Jairazbhoy to join the Asian Studies Department at Windsor University in Canada as teaching assistant and archivist. A year later she joined Wesleyan University (Conn.) in the USA where she pursued her studies in Indian music and ethnomusicology, gaining her Ph.D. degree in 1976. Her dissertation was on 'Tabla and the Banaras Gharana'.

In 1976 she went to India and spent three years studying the tabla and doing research in Indian music and culture. During her stay she was the secretary of the Pandit Ram Sahai Sangit Vidyalaya (Varanasi), where she ran the music and dance classes and organised concerts and conferences. On her return to the UK she spent a year at the National Association for Asian Youth in Southall as their Curriculum Development Officer and has since been a Senior Lecturer in music at Dartington College of Arts in Devon. Her work includes the running of two training courses she has developed in Indian music. She is also very active in the area of multicultural education, gives in-service training and workshops nationally and has written for *Multicultural Teaching.*

Dr Shepherd founded the Pandit Ram Sahai Sangit Vidyalaya in 1986 with Pandit Sharda Sahai. It is a charitable trust aiming to contribute to the development of Indian music and dance education in the UK. Its main activity is currently the administration of music and dance examinations for an Indian examination Board at different centres in the UK.